THE
CLOSET
HANGING

Also by Tony Fennelly
The Glory Hole Murders

THE
CLOSET
HANGING

Tony Fennelly

AN AUTHORS GUILD BACKINPRINT.COM EDITION

The Closet Hanging

All Rights Reserved © 1987, 2000 by Tony Fennelly

AN AUTHORS GUILD BACKINPRINT.COM EDITION

Published by iUniverse.com, Inc.

For information address:
iUniverse.com, Inc.
620 North 48th Street, Suite 201
Lincoln, NE 68504-3467
www.iuniverse.com

Originally published by Carroll & Graf

The author wishes to thank Diplomat Music for permission
to quote, on page 109, the lines from the song entitled
A House Is Not A Home, Hall David.

ISBN: 0-595-14237-0

Printed in the United States of America

Dedicated to Richard Catoire
(Who else?)

Prologue
Sunday, March 5th

"Lookey here! It's true what they say about a hanged man."

"What's that, Duffy?"

"I heard where a guy gets a big ol' hard-on when he's hanged. Just like this poor clown. What was his name, chief?"

"It's difficult to recognize him, but his maid says the victim was one Brad Rutledge. And I'd rather you didn't make light of it."

Lieutenant Frank Washington of the N.O.P.D. backed out of the cedar closet and turned away from its sole occupant suspended grotesquely from a well-constructed clothes pole.

The still-warm corpse was fully dressed but for shorts and trousers, which lay heaped in the corner. The late Mr. Rutledge's head was cocked at a crazy angle by a tightened yard of clothes line, and his face was bulging and discolored. Florsheim-shod toes pointed to the firm parquet tiles scant inches away as though desperately seeking a grounding. A small three-legged stool had rolled just out of reach.

"Sure, we got to be respectful and all that," Duffy conceded. "But I'm thinkin' that I saw this guy somewhere before. Lookin' a lot fresher, natcherly."

"I would imagine so." Washington recalled that the dead man had been a prominent attorney, with his own real estate development corporation. "There's no apparent reason for suicide."

"Suicide? Nah, he just wanted to whack off. That's why his pants were down." The young patrolman pointed unnecessarily. "I saw this report on Channel Six. See a guy ties a rope around his own neck to cut off oxygen so he'll come better."

"Yes, I'm acquainted with the phenomenon. Forensic experts call it 'autoerotic asphyxia.' "

Washington made a quick survey of the nineteenth-century Georgian house with its fourteen-foot ceilings. If Rutledge had lived in one of those shoddy new condos, with low ceilings and flimsy mountings, he couldn't have died this way. Not by hanging.

"So there the guy is, gettin' all ready to make time with himself." Duffy offered. "But the stool he's standin' on turns over and that's it." He pulled his tie up sharply, crossed his eyes, and stuck out his tongue for dramatization. "Agh agh, ghack!"

Washington frowned and closed his note pad.

"I don't like it."

"Who would?"

"You were in the Navy, right?"

"Four goddamn miserable years. Why?"

"I don't know much about knots."

"Never met a black who did—no offense."

"What kind is that around his neck?"

Duffy moved in closer and squinted. "Slip bowline, I guess. Yeah, good knot. Why?"

"Looks to me like the fixed part of the loop is here on the man's right and the sliding end is on his left."

"You got it."

"But a right-handed man would hold the sliding part in his right."

Duffy closed his eyes and tightened an imaginary noose.

"Okay, so the poor sucker was a southie."

"No, I don't think so. Look, he's wearing his watch on his left. . . . On second thought, better not look."

Duffy looked anyway. "Now I remember where I saw

this Brad Rutledge. Just last week he was on TV mouthing off about casino gambling."

Washington turned sharply. "Gambling? Pro or con?"

"Pro, definitely. To hear him tell it, New Orleans'll sink right into the Gulf without a casino."

"So that's the connection."

"What?"

The lieutenant walked through the living room past the two uniforms on patrol and the chattering Latin maid who had just stopped by to collect the dry cleaning and found something she never expected.

The floor-to-ceiling casement windows afforded him a wide view of Nine Hundred block, Dauphine Street, quiet and residential most days because the noisier bars and jazz clubs are on Bourbon, one block over. But this being Sunday, the tourists were swarming even up this far, singing and dancing in their souvenir T-shirts.

He turned to the bedroom. "Duffy, you grew up around here. So tell me, don't the Sinclairs own this building?"

"This and maybe seven others in the neighborhood. Why?"

"Because now already we have a lead."

"Excuse me for bein' stupid, chief. What lead?"

"Matt Sinclair."

"What's that fag got to do with anything?" The patrolman looked back to the physical evidence and whistled low. "I still can't get over it. This here guy has the biggest hard-on I ever saw."

"Oh, shut up, Duffy. It isn't doing him a bit of good."

Chapter 1
Sunday, March 5th

When I woke up in the middle of Jackson Square with a ringing headache and a crowd of pitying faces around me, I knew it had happened again.

Damn!

One of the faces, a plump black female's, hovered closer than the others, as though on guard.

"Don't try to move yet."

I didn't really think I could, but pride compelled me to make the attempt.

She turned to the whisperers and gapers around us.

"Y'all can go now. You see he's all right."

And the crowd obeyed, murmuring and shuffling back to their daily lives, looking only briefly behind them. The exhibition was over.

The woman offered a sturdy arm to hoist me into a sitting position.

"Sorry I didn't have any mint."

"Mint? What for?"

"Never mind," she soothed. "Do you have seizures often?"

"More often than I'd like."

She smiled and held out her hand this time. "I'm Lilly Coleman. I work at Charity."

I took it gratefully. "Matt Sinclair. And I'm glad there was a professional on the scene."

"You should be. Nobody else around here half knew what was going on."

"Lovely people but misinformed, right? I'll bet one kind soul wanted to call an ambulance."

"Actually, three volunteered."

"Then some well-wisher tries to jam a comb between my teeth and chip perfectly good incisors."

"They had a Popsicle stick this time. But the way your head was pitched all the way back, I knew you couldn't swallow your tongue. So I told them they should just clear a space and leave you be. Then I watched to make sure you kept breathing."

"For which I'm forever in your debt. How long was I out?"

"Five minutes. If it had gone over ten, I would have called the paramedics." She tapped her watch. "It was a strange thing, Matt. I noticed you at first because you came tearing through the park toward the river like it was a matter of life and death. Then you just rocked back and fell down."

A big hurry to get where? I was going to meet . . . Brad Rutledge? That name sprang into my fuzzy mind. No, it was Robin. I was to lunch with him at George D's. He would be waiting. Why would I have been going toward the river? The restaurant was the other way.

I always black out after a seizure, so whatever happened immediately before is lost. I reached into my billfold to get her a business card. "I run a furniture store when I'm not out here thrashing around on the pavement."

Mrs. Coleman examined it at arm's length while I fumbled for my pen.

"New Traditions? That's a fine shop, but I never could afford to buy anything there."

"You can now." I took the card back and printed in tiny letters, "Lilly Coleman—40% off anything she wants, Matt," and returned it to her.

"Oh, no. I couldn't take anything like this."

I closed her hand around it. "Please. You saved me a very expensive and humiliating ambulance ride."

*   *   *

When I finally found my way out to our regular table at George D's, Robin was already on his second Bananas Foster. The latest issue of *Impact* was propped against the sugar bowl and turned to the classified ads.

He waved giddily. "Listen to this personal, Matty. It says, 'Stern master seeks naked body slave. Must have intense psychological surrender from groveling masochist. Dog collar training, leather submission, naked domestic service.' Isn't that fabulous!"

"Super. Does 'Stern Master' give an address? Maybe I can hurry over there after dessert. Give me a menu."

"You're not taking this seriously enough. Do you want me to read you about 'Hot Hung Bodybuilder'?"

"No, I do not."

I didn't really need the menu. I always order the same thing on Sunday, and the waiter swooped in with a Bloody Mary while my luncheon companion kept the paper in front of his face and nattered on.

"Here's 'Gay white male, five foot ten, one hundred and forty pounds, blue eyes, mustache, seeks man with similar physical features for jerk-off partner.' "

"Why doesn't he just get a mirror? Shut up and pass me some of your coffee."

He shook his spoon in reproach.

"Our date was for one sharp, Matty."

"Unavoidable delay. I had a seizure in Jackson Square."

"Tsk tsk. By the fountain?"

"Um. Yes."

"It's better by the fountain. No grass stains. You must have looked funny."

"Hilarious."

The adorable though insensitive Robin has been my housemate for over eight months and has failed to say anything remotely sensible in all that time. But he has big brown eyes, soft golden curls, and that energy and enthusiasm found only among nineteen-year-old airheads.

And he gives the best blow jobs in all Christendom.

"Hey!" It just occurred to him. "You haven't fallen down in years. Why now?"

"I can't imagine. Didn't I take my medicine last night?"

"Sure, when 'the pathological liar' was on TV. Well, you got here in time to pay the bill, so it makes no difference."

"Of course it makes a difference. I've got to find out why it happened."

"Why it happened? You have epilepsy. So what?"

"So I can't drive until I'm sure it won't happen again."

This thought merited laying down his spoon. "Gee, that's right. Suppose you were just tooling along at sixty miles an hour down I-Ten and all of a sudden you conked out."

"Exactly."

"You might *total* the Mercedes. And then your insurance would *double*."

"No, it wouldn't." So he's stupid. We all have our flaws. "Anyhow, what's the issue? I couldn't have been more than ten minutes late."

"You kidding?" Robin showed me his watch. "It's after two. I thought I had been stood up right here in front of everybody. First I tried to brazen it out and just stalled over the menu, but then . . ."

As he blithered away about his girlish embarrassment, I tried to reconstruct the events of the afternoon. Where had I been between one o'clock and two? Why was I in such a hurry when Mrs. Coleman saw me? And headed in the wrong direction.

Brad Rutledge. Why did that name keep intruding?

I was distracted from my ruminations when the proprietor, George D. himself, bustled over with a pot of coffee and chicory. He poured me a cup and refilled Robin's. "Evening, Matty. You like the way I redid the entranceway?"

"Only the pieces I sold you."

"Don't be a bitch. I have a great eye for decoration. Look around you." He shrugged one shoulder elaborately to indicate his pride of handsome, muscular young employees hurrying about with their trays and menus.

"No question," I agreed most heartily. "You've an unerring eye for male pulchritude."

"And they're checked out, every one." George D. waved his pot around in a full circle. "Before a man comes to work here he has to be tested for AIDS and get a clean bill of health."

"What for? AIDS isn't transmitted through food handling."

"I know. But I always let my waiters screw me." He invited himself to join us, took a chair, and thrust out his left lapel, which held a little gold lingerie pin. "See this? Where's yours?"

"My what?"

"This is the latest accessory, my dear. The safety pin helps me to avoid all those nasty diseases that are going around."

"Indeed? I'd love to see it work."

"How it works is, I just wear it on my lapel like this. Then when I go out cruising in bars and bathhouses, all the queens around will see it and understand that I'm only interested in *safe* sex."

He didn't know how ridiculous that sounded, so I didn't try to tell him. Myself, I've taken to carrying a Trojan in my wallet like a schoolboy.

He buttered the last of Robin's croissants and signaled the waiter for more.

"Matty, while you're here let's talk turkey about the legalized gambling bill. I have to tell you that I'm in favor of bringing a casino to the New Orleans area."

"Too bad, George. I'm fighting it with every muscle and sinew."

"So I'm aware. All the old money in the city is ganged up against this bill, and you're the ringleader."

"Wrong. My name only gets in the papers because I'm handling the legal side. If we have a ringleader at all it's Edwina Devon."

"I'm not worried about Edwina Devon. A guy from our side is working on her. You know Bill Oakes?"

"I wish I did, but I've never had the extreme pleasure."

"Well, he's Brad Rutledge's partner."

There was that name again.

I said, "Bill Oakes is a real estate developer these days. But he used to play defense for the New Orleans Saints."

"For the 'New Orleans Potatoes', you mean. The team is always in the cellar." George made a face. "I'm sure Bill would like to forget those years. Anyhow he's about to develop that new casino gambling complex into the biggest attraction in the South." The waiter delivered our croissants and George cleared a place for them. "If only you weren't holding everything up. You and your goddamn ace in the hole."

"It's a matter of what's best for our city. Yours and mine."

"Yeah? Then just please listen to some reason." A chubby finger poked the sugar bowl. "Our city, yours and mine, has unemployment over thirteen percent. There's not enough money in the treasury to run the city, and we've already got a nine percent sales tax, the highest in the country."

"Not to mention the most repressive. Since the poor man has to spend everything he makes, the burden falls most heavily on him."

"And it's going to get worse yet, because our biggest taxpayer, the oil industry, has gone completely to hell. We *need* the casino."

"I heard those same arguments presented on behalf of the World's Fair. How many millions did that debacle cost the taxpayers last time anyone looked?"

He harrumphed and tried another tack.

"You're a Sinclair. So you just can't understand what it's like for some poor slob who has to go out and work."

"Hold on there, George. I've made my own living since I was seventeen years old."

"But you never had to: that's the difference."

"Tell you what, George." I uncapped my fountain pen. "I will personally invest some of my filthy old money in a plane ticket for you."

"For me?"

"Round trip to Atlantic City. You go talk to some of the restauranteurs up there. Ten years ago those misguided wretches spoke up for the casinos as vehemently as you do now."

"Yeah? And they got them, too."

"But no new business. Because the casino hotels don't want their gamblers leaving the premises. So they provide restaurant meals at a lower price than you can—and every other product and service, too. Conventioneers who used to go whoring down Bourbon Street will never see the outsides of their hotels."

George sighed a long sigh. "I'm just going to take the time to rethink this. . . . You'd really pay for a plane ticket?"

I took out my checkbook. "Call Delta and book your flight."

"In the interest of research, maybe I could break away for just one day. And get in some gambling."

At that point the town crier, Les Bordon, minced through the entranceway. On spotting me at my usual table, he accelerated his ladylike gait and flounced on over.

"Matt. Oh my, I have *terrible* news. The police have just found Brad Rutledge's body!"

"Dead?" Robin asked naïvely.

"Of course dead! He hanged himself in his own closet. Tied a rope around his neck, climbed up on a stool, and kicked it away. He looked *awful!*"

"That's a shame," I allowed, making a note in the ledger part of my Whitney personal checkbook.

My nonreaction seemed to affect him more than the original discovery.

"Doesn't that shock you?"

"Not at all. I never cared much for Brad, even back in law school. Besides, I haven't run into him in months."

"The heck you haven't!" Les shrilled. "This very morning I saw you in heated conversation with the dude on the corner of Royal and Dumaine. He was flapping some piece of paper in your face, and, my goodness, you looked like you wanted to *strangle* him!"

Dr. Nicolas Wright, the internist who serves as "gynecologist" for most gays of my acquaintance, has his practice way up by the lake. But as my epilepsy is permanent and unalterable, all he can do for me is renew my prescriptions, so I don't see him professionally more than twice a year.

Nick doesn't keep office hours on Sunday, so this afternoon it was mine to go directly to his home in Gentilly. I climbed the slope of his manicured front lawn and banged the brass door knocker (the ring in the lion's nose) more loudly than was fit.

There was a scuttling noise within, then the sound of the peephole being uncovered before the door was opened at last by Nick's companion of ten years, the very fastidious Sammie McKenna.

"Oh, hi there, Matty. You're just in time for din-din. I'll put anther steak on."

I followed his Armani-clad behind into the immaculate living room, gorgeously decorated in the French colonial style. I knew that Sam did all the housework himself and wondered if I should drag Robin inside for a lesson in domestic responsibility.

Sam was not only Nick's housekeeper-companion but also his adopted son. This civil sleight-of-hand is the only way most gays can establish a legal relationship for insurance and inheritance purposes. As an occasionally practicing lawyer, I've filed several such petitions for gay couples in lieu of marriage.

"Thank you, Sam. But this is really a professional call."

"S'okay. The doctor is in." The man of the house came out of the kitchen then to greet me, wearing only shorts that emphasized his avoirdupois. Nick is butch and doesn't have to be good-looking.

"Nick, there's something wrong with me."

"Always was, Matty. Step into my office."

My internist's home office is a well-lighted octagonal room with southern, northern, and eastern explosures. Sam had decorated it in "frontier doctor" style with tall oaken bookshelves, rustic desk and chairs, and a gun rack over the mantelpiece.

The heir to Hippocrates and Milburn Stone rocked back in his swivel chair. "So what's new?"

"I just had another seizure."

He was professionally unperturbed, tapping a sterling silver fountain pen on the glass desk plate.

"That's funny. Where?"

"Very funny. Right smack in the middle of Jackson Square, where everybody and his wife could suck Popsicles and enjoy the performance."

"Did you hurt yourself?"

"No, it felt good."

Nick gave me a distracted once-over, then just shrugged.

"So long as you weren't driving . . . or operating heavy equipment. Skipped your medicine, huh?"

"Never. I take it with my toothpaste every night without fail."

"Yeah. Well, you have to keep a certain amount of phenobarbital in your system."

"Ninety milligrams a day. Just what the witch doctor ordered."

"That should be enough for a man your size. We don't want to get you addicted." He reached for his pad of prescription blanks with the Rx prayer to Zeus in the upper right-hand corners. "So we'll just continue with same dosage. But if it happens again, we'll think about increasing it. The Dilantin, too. Keep taking the same two hundred milligrams twice a day."

I sat on his leather couch. Real leather, of course. I smelled it.

"There's another problem, Nick. I can't remember what happened just before I fell down."

Nick scribbled on two of the blanks, writing in a vertical column because he's a *gaucheur*, left-handed.

"Sure. Some amnesia is inevitable."

"I know, but I seem to have lost a whole hour, and I've got to get it back."

"Most of it will come back gradually. But not the few minutes just before you fell down. Those brain cells were inactivated by the electrical activity."

"The last thing I remember is leaving the shop to meet Robin for lunch. It must have been around twelve forty-five. After that I woke up in Jackson Square, going in the wrong direction, an hour late for lunch—and thinking about Brad Rutledge."

Nick looked up sharply. "Poor Brad? I just heard about him on the radio."

"Bad news gets right out."

"He was one of my patients. Also, I invested a fortune with the man's development corporation. So killing himself was a dirty trick, which I take personally."

"You know Brad. Sneaky and underhanded to the very end."

"Did you see him before he did it?"

"Who knows? All I recalled of Brad was his name and the fact that I had some important business with him."

"In that case, I can only suggest that you ask possible witnesses to fill in the gaps for you. By the way, don't drive until we're sure this thing is under control again."

"Wouldn't dream of it. Robin brought me here."

"Robin? I wouldn't trust that boy to drive a lawnmower down the City Park fairway. But it's your neck."

Chapter 2
Monday Morning, March 6

Sigrid turned the dust rag around in her hand several times, as though trying to discern its function before tentatively applying it to the arm of a chair. Then she stepped back to judge the effect. Not much.

I bought this Queen Anne–style house on Esplanade back in 1974. The second and third stories are given over to tenants, so Robin and I have only our first floor apartment to keep up. Even so, I've gone through dozens of cleaning women through the years. Unfortunately, most of our "household technicians" have spent more time at the kitchen table paging through tabloids than on their feet earning an honest dollar.

Sigrid Wilson, though, may be the worst even of that low company. I've given Robin charge of her so he can learn some management skills. But, being a Yankee liberal, he considers it immoral to give orders to a servant, and adds the charge of racism if the servant happens to be black.

So during this particular breakfast, he never looked up from his *Times-Picayune*.

"Look here, Matty, the Audubon Zoo wants to mate its grizzly bear."

"I'm all dated up this week."

"They're shooting the bear with a tranquilizer to ship him across the lake. Your friend Cowboy Eisenhardt is supposed to supervise the mating."

"Cowboy's a natural Cupid."

Robin was stuffing down pancakes as he read, a

14

thousand calories' worth. The erp. "And here's some interesting news. The sheriff got arrested for drunk driving again."

"That's not news." I had half a grapefruit and a bowl of Total in front of me, no more than 300 calories.

"Okay, here's another item. They're selecting jurors for the Governor's trial."

"What's the latest on that circus? Yesterday, Governor Crowley objected because they excused the illiterates."

Robin folded his paper on page three. "I remember what he told the reporters: 'Someone doesn't have to read to know a man is innocent'."

"But it helps in determining that he's guilty."

"They've got themselves a real cross-section so far. One juror is a wife beater; another accidentally killed his best friend. Now there's a shoplifter dropped in for good measure."

"And what did the Governor say about that menage?"

" 'A jury of my peers.' "

"I believe it. He'd better keep his Cajun wits about him, too. Some spoilsport may ask him where he gets all his gambling money."

"Ooh!" Robin jerked back as though he'd been slapped. "Here's *your* name in Betty's column!"

"I'd rather not hear it."

"But it's fantastic! 'Eminently eligible Matt Sinclair seen squiring La beauteous Edwina Devon. June wedding to come?'

"Hey, wait a minute!" Robin squawked this out in the tone of a startled parrot. "What the heck does she mean, 'June wedding'?"

"Betty knows better."

"But she writes about you just like you were straight."

"Because rich, handsome bachelors don't make good copy if they're gay." I poured myself a cup of excellent coffee. "I could gratify the entire Saints offensive line in the Superdome at half-time, and Betty and her kind would still rave on about how 'eligible' I am."

Nonetheless he seized upon the excuse to pout. "You have been seeing an awful lot of that fish lately."

"Only in the interests of the common good. We're working together against the casino bill." My coffee was too hot. I drank it anyway. "Of course, Edwina is smart, beautiful, and a delightful tennis partner, but I wouldn't have a chance with her anyhow. She's dating a scrumptious ex-football player named Billy Oakes."

Robin tipped his chin up. "Oh yeah? Well, I happen to know that Bill is working for the *opposite* of the common good. He wants the casino."

"*Now* he does. But Edwina is working on him."

"Oh, I get it. She's a spy."

"A saboteuse."

Robin finished the last of the pancakes and tapped his lips with his napkin. "That was very good. The second helping will be even better." He repaired to the kitchen to recommence his never-ending cycle of cooking and eating.

Sigrid pulled out the vacuum and managed to turn on the blower, spraying dust all over the living room. I leaped from the table to wrest the appliance out of her hand.

"I'm sorry, Mister Matt. I jes' don't know where my head is at."

"Don't look too long."

"See, I been so upset."

"What you want this to do is suck in the dirt, not blow it out. The switch goes this way."

"You know what? My neighbor done call the welfare office to tell 'em I was workin'. She jes' bein' dirty."

"And inaccurate." I took the path of least resistance and vacuumed up the mess myself. Sigrid was kind enough to watch without stepping on the hose.

"My social worker gonna come 'round investigatin' an' make trouble. I pray to God they don't find out how much I be makin' and ax for my food stamps back."

"You pray about that?"

"I know He'll he'p me."

I moved a chair aside to vacuum behind it and imagined the Lord of the universe putting His infinite powers to work as accessory to a food stamp scam.

"You don' know how hard it be, Mr. Matt. Willie, he want a gold tooth for his birt'day. He gon' be thirteen. An' the dentist done tol' me it'll take a hunnert fifty dollars. I don' know how I'm gon' make it."

"Some luxuries have to be denied."

"But Willie won't understan', 'cause William, he got him one."

She named her two older sons William and Willie. At first I assumed that this was in case one son Will was slain in the line of duty—holding up a gas station, for example. She would still have a spare.

But there was another reason for the redundancy.

Like others in her social circle, Sigrid has never been in a position to give her children their fathers' last names. So she makes do with their first. And her two oldest sons were both misbegotten by vagrants named William. The daughters, typically, are bestowed Christian names that aren't Christian at all but soft pagan sounds like Latasha, Kaneesha, and Saleesha, evoking exotic places and tropical passions, beautiful names being the only wealth available to a woman of Sigrid's class.

I believe she is pregnant yet again, but perhaps she hasn't noticed yet. The proud father would be one Lewis Wofford, whose presence can be discerned only by the noise of the rap version of "Gilligan's Island" emitting from his ghetto blaster out on the sidewalk. I won't allow his likes in my house or even inside the iron gate.

"I saw Travis's daddy las' week."

Travis is her third- or fourth-born. He, too, is banned from the premises, because the boy is hyperactive from a daily overdose of sugar and salt and enjoys pulling down draperies.

"Glory be. I thought Travis's father had disappeared."
I handed her the broom. What harm could she do with
a broom?

"Oh no, we sees him alla time. When we lines up to
git cheese, he's one o' them that passes it out."

"It pays to have connections." I showed her the dust-
pan and pointed to a light coating of dust she had left
in the foyer. "Try these on that."

Sigrid boasts six children who avoid school by day and
run the streets at night. Among them they have six
different fathers, one of whom is doing life plus ninety-
nine in Leavenworth. Oddly enough, the only one who
has acted anything like a parent is the poor mucker in
stir. Innis makes dolls in the prison shop and sends
them along at Christmas.

Another of Sigrid's infelicitous prayers is that poor
Innis will be let out of prison. What she should really
do is try to get the other five in.

"Someone is at the front door," I informed her well-
larded posterior.

"I didn't hear no bell."

"Visual aid." I pointed to my Boxer, Blanch, who was
standing in the foyer, ears up and rear end wagging
furiously.

"Mus' be a white man. She ain't barkin'."

Our visitor, Lieutenant Frank Washington, doesn't
fit that description, but he has a white man's love of
dogs and they sense it. He paused on entering to give
Blanche a friendly scratch behind the ears and she
retired to her rug, content. When Frank came to join
us at the table, I poured him a cup of coffee, not fool
enough to trust Sigrid with the task.

"You'll be glad you came, just for this."

He sipped carefully, getting behind the steam. "Rii-
ight! This might just be the best coffee I ever tasted!"

"That's a blend of Guatemala and Antigua beans. I
roasted it myself last night and ground it this morning."

"The freshness makes quite a difference. I'll just sleep with my eyes open this week."

As Sigrid sauntered into the kitchen and tried to figure out what the mop was for, he watched her lack of progress over his cup rim.

"My wife is looking for help. How is your Miss Wilson doing?"

"I wish I had ten just like her."

"Really?"

"Sure. Among them all, they might do the work of one normal person."

"That's what I thought. What do you keep her around for? She's hardly decorative."

"Hardly. But she has kids and needs the money."

"I think you're constrained by this Old South plantation mentality, Mars' Matt. You see yourself as the benevolent slave holder."

"That's not fair."

"But it doesn't fly under the new rules, see. If you owned Sigrid, you could flog the bitch and make her work. But times being what they are, you don't own her and so you don't have to feed her fat ass."

"In a world where the fittest survive, someone has to take responsibility for the unfit."

"Don't waste your charity on her, Matty. I know the breed. She gets"—he lowered his voice and addressed the coffee—"a woman like that gets welfare, food stamps, subsidized housing, utilities paid . . . And don't think her boyfriends aren't contributing."

"I concede on those issues. But isn't it due to cultural conditioning? The woman doesn't know any better."

What I didn't say was that I felt a special responsibility for Sigrid since one Saturday night some three months previous when I rescued her from further shame and defilement.

It was nearly two A.M. in Freed's art gallery on St. Phillip Street. Nat Freed had kindly lent me some paintings for a display set, and I was up in his second floor storeroom packing water colors. The gallery's staff had long dispersed to their various trysts and parties, so I was all alone, driving nails into flat crates, when I heard faint sounds of distress from outside. Carrying my hammer to the window, I looked down through the fire escape to the alley below. There were featured three black people in what seemed to be a lusty orgy amid the garbage cans, piles of oyster shells, and stinking shrimp heads.

Central to the tableau was a kneeling woman whose dingy striped sweater had been pulled up nearly to her throat, exposing large, pendulous breasts that heaved in the dim light. Her short and tight skirt had been raised similarly to bare obese hips and thighs. A lanky young man with a shaggy afro knelt behind her to avail himself of the latter opportunity. Having unsheathed his member, he was now thrusting same between the jiggling buttocks in a slow and rhythmic motion, as though simultaneously listening to a laid-back blues number. At the same time, a slight-built youth of high school age squatted in front of the woman, flicking his tongue into her slack mouth and kneading her soft brown breasts to the same beat established by his elder.

I was backing away to leave them to their sport when I glimpsed a flash of steel under the alley light. Only then did I see that the man in the rear held a foot-long shiv to the woman's belly, moving it back and forth against the plump flesh, lazily directing her movement with the point.

I realized that the victim's bra had been removed and used to bind her arms, and her dark eyes were bugged out with fear. The faint bleating I'd heard was the only sound she'd dared make as the obscene dance continued.

I hefted my hammer experimentally and found it too light and unevenly balanced for my purpose.

The sharp edge of the rapist's blade was directly under the woman's gut. If any less than totally dis-

abled, he might just disembowel her out of sheer mean-
ness. I needed something heavy and sure.

I ducked back into the room and put my hand on a
more appropriate missile, a thirty-pound iron copy of
Moore's "Woman," crept out across the fire escape,
aimed it directly at the knifer's third vertabra, and let it
drop. With a dull grunt, he collasped against his victim,
knocking her and his henchman over together. The
weapon clattered to the bricks as I hurtled down the
steel ladder and launched myself into the confusion,
hammer swinging.

"Okay, scumbags! Let's try it again with a man!"

I shouted loud enough to alert everyone in the faubourg if anyone cared. Of course no one did and I
knew that I was on my side all alone, but the noise had
routing power just the same.

The younger punk scrambled out from underneath
the melee and tore down St. Phillip Street like a man
on fire. The rapist took another few seconds to pull his
head together but, having no taste for a fair fight
either, he also adopted a legs-save-body strategy and
scuttled out after his companion.

The woman waved a fist and shrieked at their fleeing
backs. "Motherfuckers! My ol' man Lewis'll git you!"
She wagged her head at me. "An' he will, too. Donchu
worry. I knows where dey mama stay."

I respectfully pulled her skirt down behind her before working on the knot in the bra. "I can drive you to
the police station." That suggestion was never even
answered. I'd only made it for form anyhow.

She shook out the bra, then seemed to forget it, as she
didn't try to put it back on or even pull her sweater down.

"Thanks, mister. You done real good for me. I cain't
give you any money, but"—she lifted her fat arms—"I
can pay you in trim if you want."

When I realized which medium the poor creature
was offering, I was horrified. Hadn't she taken enough
degradation for one evening? But then I was touched

by her presumption that the referred-to asset had any value.

"No!" I said too quickly, then amended it. "I'm gay, you see. I only go with men."

She looked puzzled at that. "A fruit? Oh well, you cain't he'p it. Can you?"

"That's right. I can't."

"Too bad." She pulled down her sweater at last, then dug around for her purse. I conducted a search and eventually found it for her, leaning up against a plastic sack of garbage.

"Those niggers took all my food stamps. How'm I gonna feed my chillen, mister? How?"

She asked this accusingly, as though it were my problem. I automatically reached for my wallet.

"Here's twenty. That should keep you in beans and rice for a few days."

She looked at it indifferently. "Ain't enough there. I got six."

That's when I offered her a job cleaning and she accepted it with well-disguised gratitude.

And now Washington was saying, "If you coddle the likes of Sigrid, you're only subsidizing the deterioration of a culture."

"The idea is to impart some old-fashioned values— Puritan work ethic."

"You'll never do it."

"Maybe not, but I've got to try. How about some breakfast? Robin's in there making pancakes."

Frank, who like me is pushing forty, didn't dare indulge. He shook his head sadly and then rewarded himself with an extra teaspoon of sugar in his coffee.

I argued from another angle. "I remember when I was a boy, my mother would take in some raw girl from the country who couldn't even use a fork. But with patience and training she would make a fine lady's maid out of her."

"Is that so? Well, thirty years ago your 'raw girl from the country' was probably a superior person to begin with. Racist policies had trapped her family in poverty and denied her schooling, so she was dying to improve herself." He took a long swallow, probably needing the caffeine. "But now we have education and opportunity for everyone who wants them. Your raw girl wouldn't have to settle for lady's maid today. She would probably be public relations director at Odeco."

"Spoken like a true Republican."

Frank is the same complexion as Sigrid Wilson but would claim nothing else in common with her. Some of his ancestors, "ladies and gentlemen of color," owned property and people before the war. And his great-great grandfather, Louis le Blanc, fought for the Confederacy because he didn't want to lose his slaves. Following haughty family tradition, Frank's maternal grandfather, Marcel le Blanc, was prime mover of the Autocrat Club back in the thirties, when its admissions policy was the most exclusive in New Orleans. Members could be no darker than a grocery bag, and a fine-tooth comb had to pass through their hair (light-skinned Negroes being the most color-conscious people anywhere).

Frank's mother, Delphia, was disowned by her fine quadroon family when she defied all convention to marry a penniless and very black jazz pianist, "Keys" Washington.

All of New Orleans remembers how Keys used to make the room rock during the colored half of the show at the 809 Club. (That was twenty-five years ago, when it was still illegal for whites and blacks to share a stage.) But one more excellent musician in a city full of the finest can't make a good living even today. And it was worse before integration. Delphia was fair enough of complexion to get a sales job at Maison Blanche, but there was never much money in the Washington household. So Frank had to work his way through college and now can boast that he's a "self-made man." But it was his parents who made him. Breeding tells.

Today, in this era of Grace Jones, there is much weeping and gnashing of teeth among the high-color patricians as their sons and daughters, insisting that blacker is more beautiful, drag home dark-skinned friends and lovers who wouldn't have been allowed in the front door a few years ago.

Frank drained his cup and pushed it away. "But never mind. I didn't come by for a symposium on sociology." He pulled a length of clothes line from his coat pocket and held it out. "I recall that you used to work as a pipeline rigger."

"Summers during college and law school."

"How about making me a slip bowline."

"My pleasure." I made a regular bowline around the standing part and tossed it back to him.

He slid the line approvingly.

"I can't tie knots."

"Of course you can't."

This, too, may be cultural conditioning. I've seen otherwise knowledgeable blacks try to dog off a load, and it's a study in futility. They use up fifty feet of rope making five hundred assholes around every post, beam, and horizontal they can reach and finish with a granny knot. Then when they've waved the mess up and the crane slacks off on it, you'd better dive for a hatch, because that load is coming *down*! And you don't ever want to be in the way of running cable, whipping and snaking and making sparks all over the deck. In seconds it will demolish all the prefab storage shacks and have 400-pound oil drums crashing like bowling pins. And any man caught topside will be cut in a minimum of two pieces. All for the want of one good knot.

In less than five seconds you can tie a clove hitch with a safety that will hold any load. But some men never learn the basics.

"Tying knots is a specialized skill," Washington said.

"Not so unusual in the oil patch."

"I'm only bringing this up because a certain adversary of yours was hanged with just such a knot yesterday."

"You mean Brad Rutledge?"

"And there's another connection. You own the building he lived and died in."

"More correctly, my mother owns it and I oversee the management. Anyhow, why is Homicide interested in the case. The news broadcast reported Brad committed suicide."

"That's as much as we gave the media. It might also be taken for an accident."

"A man accidentally climbs up on a stool, fastens a rope around his neck, then kicks away the stool?"

"It's not a pleasant subject, but you're sure to hear of it eventually. Autoerotic asphyxia."

"I understand the Latin well enough, but the term eludes me."

"Some people believe pressure on the carotid arteries can heighten . . . um . . . enjoyment." Frank made an effort to sound clinical. "What happens is the . . . the onanist loops a rope around his neck, pulls it tight, and . . . well . . . he masturbates then and there."

"Shocking. And you seem to have an aficionado's knowledge of this sport, Frank. From personal experience?"

"You kidding? Is there any black man in the South who would ever put a rope around his own neck?"

"I wouldn't imagine."

"We don't even like *ties*. Anyhow, there are between five hundred and a thousand such incidents each year in this country alone. And the coroner of any large city can tell you of cases where they found some poor loser hanged in his own bedroom closet with his pants down."

"Funny that I've never read any obits to that effect."

"Naturally not. In the interests of decency, the authorities pull the pants back up and call it a suicide. For the sake of the family."

"All right, Lieutenant. This has been pleasant break-fast table chatter. But couldn't I have waited for the movie? Why tell me?"

"Because the case in point is different. The man, Rutledge, died with a clothes line around his neck, choked to death. But it wasn't motivated by an acrobatic libido."

"What makes you think so?"

"The stool, for one thing. If the man had no intention of hanging himself, why wouldn't he just lengthen his rope and stand on the floor."

"Suppose he did mean to hang himself?"

"Dammit, Matt. If suicide was his object, why would he take his pants off first?"

"Brad was an extremely vain man."

"It wasn't an accident or suicide, and I can prove it. I've been saving the best till last." Frank tilted back and smiled a smug self-satisfied smile. "The knot was backwards."

"Backwards?"

"The sliding part was to his left. And he was right-handed."

I took back the slip bowline and played with it. "If I were hanging myself, the knot would be to my right."

"Exactly. So as a former assistant D.A., you can see the thing stinks out loud."

"Who was last to see Brad alive?"

"You were."

"*I* was? Then there isn't much to be discovered in that direction." I grabbed the coffee pot and poured my guest another cup. "How about tracing the rope? Hardly a natural thing for a man to keep around his house—unless he makes hammocks as a side industry."

"No help there. His maid said Rutledge was into aerobics and kept the piece of clothes line handy as a skipping rope."

"He skipped rope?"

" 'For his health,' ironically. And here's another sticker

for you, the pole he was hanging from. You know that the house has fourteen-foot ceilings."

"I know every inch of the property."

"Right. Well, there's a wooden bar installed up near the top of the closet."

"I installed it myself. So a man can hang his seldom-used clothes up out of his way and have the eye-level pole free for his everyday wardrobe."

"You're an excellent carpenter, Matt. Because you made that pole strong enough to hold a hundred and forty–pound dead weight. I saw it myself."

"Thank you."

"But it couldn't have held the same hundred and forty pounds jerking violently. And poor Brad kicked quite a lot on his way out. The abrasions on the throat prove it."

"You imply that Brad was strangled then hoisted up in the closet?"

"No, he was hanged fair and square. The neck broke long-ways."

"So he was hanged somewhere else, cut down, then rehanged in the closet?"

"You like that? I've got something else for you. There is no other post or projection in the house that would have held the man's weight."

"Are we to infer that old Brad was hanged outside, maybe from a cottonwood tree where he could kick to his heart's content, then cut down, carted inside, and strung up again?"

"Not likely is it? But if that could be accomplished, who could do it better than you."

"*Moi?*"

"You own the building, know the area, have access to a key. Also there was some rivalry between you and the decedent. He had an interest in the riverfront land designated for the casino."

"Which will never be constructed. Not while I can prevent it."

"And you can prevent it. Because your mother owns the adjacent property."

"Right. My ace in the hole."

"The casino syndicate would need that acreage for a parking lot."

"And won't ever get it, I assure you."

"The syndicate must feel differently, or they wouldn't have invested so much time and money in the venture. What did Brad say to you when you met that morning?"

"I'll never know. I had a seizure right afterward."

"Yes, we heard witnesses to that occurrence. But may I play the devil's advocate?"

"Type-casting."

"Couldn't you have used your history of epilepsy as an alibi? Whatever he told you makes you madder than a hornet. So you go home with poor Brad, murder him, hang him up, then stroll back to Jackson Square, lie down, and do your thing."

"My thing being a realistic performance of a grand mal seizure?"

"Right."

"Sorry, Frank. I don't know how to give one."

"But you've—"

"Participated many times. But I've never had to look at it, thank God. I'm unconscious for the duration."

"I'll keep that in mind."

"Say, Supercop. You don't really believe that I killed Brad Rutledge?"

"No, Matt. You?" His right mustache twitched. "Hoo, certainly not! I've just got to follow every lead—like any good Supercop."

As soon as Frank left I drained my coffee and grabbed my coat. Robin bounced up unbidden.

"Where are you going so early?"

"Back to Jackson Square. I've got to figure out where I was headed when I fell down. It must have been someplace important."

"Important enough to forget your date with me? It must have been a *major crisis*. I'm going, too."

March is a good time to be in New Orleans. Mardi Gras is over. Yankees went home. The crowds have thinned.

Now the streets are peopled with conventioneers and tourists looking like either Bartles or Jaymes on off-season budgets. They toddle down Bourbon sipping Hurricanes in souvenir glasses and cursing the unexpectedly cold weather.

Our visitors from the north somehow foster the delusion that any city in the Deep South must be hot all year round. So they leave their woolies back in Iowa and lumber down the ramp at Moisant wearing only loud Hawaiian shirts and baggy shorts. Then they're the first to complain when a blast of forty-degree wind hits their bare, knobby knees. So they hump off to Maison Blanche to buy an overcoat, then step outside only to find it hot enough again for shirt-sleeves.

In New Orleans we say, "If you don't like the weather, wait a minute." This is especially true in March. This morning it was cool, around sixty, and sunny. But the temperature would warm up in the afternoon. It would be windy all day. Kite-flying season.

The St. Peter Street mall is only a ten-minute walk from the house, even with Robin trailing behind. I got my bearings at the Jackson Square entrance gate, then paced to a spot about six feet in front of the fountain.

"When I woke up I was lying right here. So I must have been going north. What's north?"

"The Cafe De Monde. You wanted some doughnuts."

"I was running like a madman to get myself some doughnuts?"

"And coffee."

"Never mind, let's walk it." We skirted around a busker who juggled knives while riding a six-foot unicycle and passed another who manipulated cards. Not too long ago, the only performers in Jackson Square were the instant portrait artists and caricaturists, but now there are as many as five shows going on at a time, including choristers and break-dancers.

We walked up Decatur Street past the home of the original Muffaletta, and Santa's Quarter's, where they sell Christmas decorations all year round. Don't ask me why.

When we passed Kelly's Liquor Store, Poupon, the gray-haired delivery man, was standing in the alleyway having a smoke. Between runs, he spends most of his day on the street, so I hailed him.

"Hey, Mr. Poupon. Did you happen to see me yesterday?"

"No, sir, Mr. Matt. Were you around?"

"I'm not sure. Did you overhear anybody talk about me? Maybe someone expected me to come by."

"Not that I recall, though Heaven knows I've been running all day. I'm too busy to listen for gossip." He removed the pencil from behind his ear. "Guess who called us? The Governor himself just ordered a case of Chivas Regal sent up to his hotel room. He's gonna be in for a long stay."

"I don't believe it," Robin challenged on his toes.

"Why not? The man's got to be at the Federal Courthouse for his trial every day. But he's still got his nights free."

"I know you're lying because I've heard Governor Crowley is a teetotaler."

"Hey boy, that crazy man has a party going day and night. He should get himself a revolving door in his suite. And my friend the bell captain told me that."

"The party never stops," I agreed. "But the only vice our governor is known not to have is drinking. You see, at some point in every young man's life, he realizes that he must choose between overindulging in liquor or in *galette*. Clement Crowley took the healthier course."

"Then why does he need all that expensive whiskey?" Robin asked.

"Good hygiene," I explained. "After His Exellency has disported with the lady of the hour, he washes his instrument in a glass of Chivas Regal."

"The Governor thinks dipping his dork in Scotch is going to prevent disease?"

"It works at least as well as a safety pin."

"I hear you." Poupon scratched his bald spot. "Since that's the subject on everybody's mind, what're you doing about AIDS?"

"Just generally behaving myself." I said. "I've long ago given up rampant promiscuity. And I stay out of the bars and the bathhouses."

"That's no place to meet nice people," Poupon agreed. "You'd do better placing a personal ad in *Impact*."

Robin giggled. "You should see the latest issue. There's this one about 'stern master.' "

Poupon nodded. "Wants intense psychological surrender?"

"Oh, you read that?"

"Hell, I *wrote* it."

Robin's jaw dropped low enough, fortunately, to keep him from laughing.

"*You're* 'stern master'?"

"I sure am." Poupon squared his shoulders. "And it was a good ad, too. I've made my first contact already."

"With whom?"

"A man who's offered to be my naked body slave. So far we've only talked on the phone, but we'll have our first encounter Wednesday night." He winked. "I've commanded him to meet me in the Vieux Carre Restaurant at *precisely* eight twenty-three. You have to be very strict from the beginning."

"Well, happy honeymoon."

"I'm going to put him through his paces all right. I'll beat him with a cat o' nine tails till he's blubbering for mercy. Then while he's groveling around there on the floor naked, I'll just—"

On that note, I bid a hasty good day and dragged my

young charge away from the delivery man's vivid game plan. Once out of earshot, Robin said, "Gee, Poupon is nice. But he doesn't fit my image of your basic 'stern master.'"

"I'm just glad I don't have to share a wall with that guy."

I stopped in the doorway of the Storyville Jazz Hall to hear some calypso while Robin skipped across the street to the French Market and bought a pound of fresh pecans, it having been a whole ten minutes since breakfast. He munched these as we walked along.

I stopped at the corner of Decatur and Esplanade.

"This is about as far as I usually go on foot. We're at the edge of the Quarter."

Robin turned to the historical building that occupied the block behind us and paced the corner. There was a sign out front in French and English, which he read aloud from the wrong side.

"Le Fort Saint Charles?"

"That's what the French called this garrison when they built it in the early days of colonization." I assumed the aspect of a tour guide. Easily, because the history of this city is Sinclair history, too. "France ceded New Orleans to Spain in seventeen sixty and the Frenchmen didn't like it. My six-times great grandfathere, Artur St. Clair, was one of the rebels who fought to overthrow the Spanish governor in sixty-nine."

"What happened to him?"

"He lost. The mercenary Governor O'Reilly executed three of his best friends right on this site. Fortunately, Artur wasn't important enough to shoot. Also, he was a practical man. So he swore allegiance to the Spanish crown and changed his name to San Claro. '*Viva el rey de España!*'"

"Sounds pretty unpatriotic to me. How come you know what your ancestors were doing over two hundred years ago?"

"I learned about most of them right up there." I

pointed. "In the third floor reading room are records of all vital statistics and legal actions since the city was founded."

"You mean anyone from New Orleans can find his great-great grandmother's birth certificate?"

"And I have all of mine, back six generations."

"Gee, could you go further if you wanted?"

"A southerner knows better than to go back too far."

"That's what I heard."

Robin is a Californian, so his idea of history is the great migration of 1956.

As we walked around to the front of the building, I continued my orientation lecture.

"After the Louisiana Purchase, this building became the U.S. Mint. Then during the war, it was the Confederate Mint. We still call it the Mint, even though it hasn't been used for that since nineteen nine. It was a federal prison for a few years, then a Coast Guard station."

"Well, what is it now?"

"Officially, the State Museum and Historical Center. But then, almost every old building around here is of historical interest. We feel close to our past in New Orleans."

After circling the block, we walked up Esplanade and turned at Dauphine Street, passing a portly gray-haired gentleman in a miniskirt and high heels.

Robin poked me in the ribs and whispered. "Look at that!"

"Look at what?"

"No stockings."

We stopped on Nine Hundred block at the house once occupied by the late Brad Rutledge. The police seal was still on the door.

We rent the Georgian single to a model tenant for $800 a month, and Brad qualified. He was neat, caused no trouble with the neighbors, and always paid on time. So however I might have disliked him as a human being, I loved him as a tenant.

"See, Robin, my grandfather, Philip Vigé, bought this house for three thousand dollars during the depression, and my mother spent her childhood here. After they moved uptown, he kept it as income property."

My protegé wasn't interested in this history either.

Milton McMann, in his wheelchair, sat across the street as he does most afternoons when it's fine. I hailed him and walked over.

"Say, Milt, did you see anyone unusual around yesterday?"

"Unusual? Christ, Matty. You're talking about the Quarter here. We got magicians, dwarves, Clowns for Jesus. Everyone is unusual!"

"How far have the cops got with the case?"

"Nowhere, Matty. I watched them all stand out in front, scratch their heads, and go inside. Ninety minutes later, they came back out and scratched their asses. They're trying to figure where Brad might have been hanged."

"What do you figure?"

"I wouldn't tell *them*."

"Tell me."

Milton backed his chair into the shade and put the brake on. "Nobody carried Brad's body into that house after he was dead. They'd have had to park a car right by the curb. And at that time of day the meter maids and tow trucks are feasting like piranha."

"Suppose they didn't drive him here?"

"Oh, come on. They carried a corpse up Dauphine Street? Even I would have noticed that. Brad walked into the house."

"They said there was nothing to hang him on inside."

"Well, there was yesterday morning; bet on it."

Chapter 3
Monday Afternoon, March 6th

When I went back to the shop, I was met at the door by Steve Hicks, my second in command.

" 'Bout time you favored us with a visit."

He waved me through with a rag socked in Old English Red Oil. (New Traditions specializes in first-quality reproductions of unaffordable antiques, and we like to treat our copies as reverently as the genuine items.)

"Think nothing of it, Steve. The least I could do."

"The very least. Matty, this heavyset black woman just came in here and bought the Chippendale dresser. And I had to give her a goddamn forty percent off because she had this card!"

He held out the one I'd given Mrs. Coleman. I took it from him and tore it in eighths. "She didn't waste any time getting over here. I'm flattered."

"How much of a profit do you expect to make with those terms?"

"None in her case, Steve. I had a seizure yesterday, and she saved me from being helped."

"Then I don't mind so much. But how the hell did it happen? You forget to take your medicine?"

"Never."

"Oh, by the way, she left you this." He tossed me something wrapped in foil.

"A twenty-five-cent chocolate mint? What's it for?"

"Search me. Hey, the ad agency sent the tape of

35

your new commercial. I'm dying to see it, but I wanted to wait for you."

"Too kind. Let's repair to my office for a private showing."

We closed the door behind us, stuck the cassette in the VHS, and sat back to watch.

"Good cinematography," he owned after a few seconds. "They make our furniture look massive. Those guys use some kind of special lens?"

"I don't ask the agency how they work. I just send them money and they send me back a commercial."

I've always had my advertising campaigns done in New York, where they turn out a slick product. I don't mean to downgrade local talent, but New Orleans–produced furniture ads tend to feature jokers in gorilla suits jumping up and down on water beds. And then there's the distinguished-looking pitchman who gets dressed up like an upholstered wing-back and introduces himself as "Mr. Chairman."

The spokeswoman in my new commercial was serene and soignée and resembled the late Babe Paley. I decided that my clientele would identify with her, or would want to.

Steve rewound the tape for another viewing.

"You going to run this on 'Couples Tell'?"

"Where else?"

"Couples Tell" is a local knock-off of "The Newlywed Game" and "Tattletales." It's an asinine offering during which a vacuous Ted Baxter type asks outrageously personal questions of heretofore dignified people. I buy time on it because the demographics are good, for some reason—but mostly because my cousin Ondine produces the show. Anyhow, nobody says I have to watch it.

Steve stretched noisily. "I sent that Pèche silver bowl over to the auction like you said. And Reverend Jack Dundy is dying to have dinner with you."

"Me and that evangelist? What could we possibly have in common?"

"Neither of you wants casino gambling, right? Should I tell him to get dipped?"

"No, tell him Wednesday night." ·

"You're very tolerant. Oops! Almost forgot to tell you, Matt. I just got an urgent phone call from the Royal Sonesta. And guess what VIP wants to pow-wow with you as soon as possible?"

"Don't keep me in suspense."

"None other than Governor Crowley himself."

I yawned. "He has time to see me?"

"Why not?"

"Because between ten and three every day, our governor is over at the Federal Courthouse fighting for his political life."

"Yeah, but trials are old stuff for him. It's still business as usual. He probably wants to wheel you and deal you."

The Royal Sonesta is a new hotel with old French flavor on the Three Hundred block of Bourbon Street, a five-minute stroll from the shop. I walked in past the lobby fountain and took the elevator up to the seventh floor tower, where two-bedroom apartments go for $500 a night. Only a public servant salaried at some $70,000 a year can afford this kind of swank.

The door to the Presidential Suite was opened by Gervis Crowley, one of the governor's trillion brothers. Gervis is the most responsible of the tribe, and it is he who takes those late night flights to Vegas with his feet on a suitcase full of cash.

He addressed me, as usual, in bad French.

"Qui ça dit, Neg'?"

I used to spend summer vacations with my cousins in Evangeline Parish so was able to reply appropriately, in a syntax that might have been even worse.

"Ça va maniere. Je contens de t'oir."

He clapped me on the back. "Glad we got a good ol' coonass here, hey, bro'?"

In response, the Governor himself strutted out of the bedroom in a tailor-made sharkskin suit. He wore large cufflinks, tie tack, collar pin, dangling watch fob, and every other personal adornment that's ever appeared in *GQ.*

"Evenin', Matt." He gripped my hand firmly."Can I git ya somethin' to drink?" He glanced down at the coffee table. "Say, I've got a glass of Chivas Regal right here."

"Uh . . . No, thank you."

"Then just sit yoreself down there an' be comfortable." And he watched me sit as though genuinely afraid that I wouldn't do it right, before starting his sales pitch.

"I'm real disappointed that we're adversaries on this here casino gambling. I know you strongly supported my re-election."

"There was no choice then. You were running against a Republican dildo."

"Still, it shows you're not afraid to get involved in public issues." He put his hand out without looking, and Gervis stuck a glass of Perrier in it. With a twist of lime.

"I just want to remind you that oil is now down near twelve dollars a barrel. And our state budget had been funded mostly by a separation tax, which was based on a price of twenty-seven a barrel."

"I've been apprised of those facts, Your Excellency." I think Crowley is the only governor in the whole United States who requests that form of address, and he so seldom gets it that his eyes glowed with the flattery. But he pressed on.

"That development has caused a crisis for every single department supported by state funds."

At this point, a tired-looking middle-aged woman came padding out of the bedroom wearing only a man's

T-shirt. I've met the first lady of the state of Louisiana and can attest that this wasn't she.

Our visitor headed for the coffee table, looking neither right nor left, and picked up the unpopular glass of Chivas Regal. She then carried her prize back to the bedroom without a word to any of us.

After she had closed the door, I said, "Tell you what, governor. Considering your famous schedule of non-stop partying, I'm surprised that you even have the energy to sit up at your desk, let alone review the fiscal situation."

"Oh, that there?" He waved an arm. "Shoot, I'm a good politician is all. I jes' want to thank ever' white lady in this state for her vote person'ly. What's wrong with that?"

"I'm glad you make the one distinction."

"Hell yeah. Bad enough I come home wit' ha'rs caught between my teeth. But them goddamn *springs*." He polished his tie clip with a cocktail napkin. "So what we got now? OPEC is lowering their prices to undersell us. The whole industry's collapsing. And we all of us depended on it—includin' you."

Including me. Most of us have worked in the patch at one time or another. I remember the oil boom of the latter sixties, when any able-bodied white male could go down to Morgan City, check into a hotel, and tell the clerk he was looking for a job. He was likely to be called off-shore before he'd got his first night's sleep— for eighty-four hours a week in the hot sun or the cold rain and all he could eat. Even at the unskilled laborer's rate of $2.20 an hour, a man could make better checks than was possible anywhere on the bank.

"So the oil's gone." His Excellency was saying. "The second industry we have around here is tourism. We got to increase our share of the vacation pie during a recession when nobody has the money to go anywhere."

"Gambling isn't the answer," I told him, "though I'll

admit this state would be a lot richer if you lost your own stakes here instead of Nevada."

"Matt, what I can't figure is how come a smart merchant like you is against my casino? Look at all the money it's gonna bring to this city. And you're a businessman first."

"High rollers headed for a casino don't stop on the way to pick up a bedroom set."

"All right, don't think of yourself then. Just listen to your conscience and the fiscal facts. We've had to cut back drastically on state agencies. The Senate is asking for a twenty percent cut in all social services. You know what that means?" He stopped for a breath and I jumped ahead of him.

"That means a lot of state workers are going to be bounced off the payroll. Welfare programs will be cut. We'll lose federal matching funds."

"You well understand."

"Better than you. People don't buy furniture when they're unemployed."

"So you ought to see why I'm fightin' for this casino. An' sweatin' an' bleedin'. It's the only plan that'll pull the state out of the fiscal mess."

"No it isn't."

"You're real smart. What's your solution then?"

"Property taxes. Ours in Louisiana are absurdly low. If we were only taxed at a millage rate comparable to most other states, we would have enough money in the treasury to do everything we're bound by conscience to do."

"Well, I never thought I'd hear that kinda talk comin' from a property owner. Most of y'all love your exemptions too much."

"I love my exemptions a lot, but I love New Orleans more. And I'll tell you that the other members of my committee are also property owners and they also agree with me."

"They willin' to reach into their deep pockets?"

"We'll take the hit, yes sir."

"Well, bless yore kind and gentle hearts. But you represent about two dozen high-minded people, and ain't one of 'em a legislator. We got the whole state to convince."

"Add to the fact that you don't want more taxes on your land in St. Landry Parish."

"No, Matt, I don't. Hell, I'll admit it for the record. I'm subject to human greed, just like anybody else."

Now the woman voter emerged from the bedroom clad in the uniform of a cocktail waitress. Apparently satisfied that her support was well-placed, she opened the door to the corridor and left the suite without comment.

The Governor seemed not to miss her.

"Your mother's property could be the most important parcel of land in our new billion-dollar casino and resort complex." He patted down an errant strand of silver hair. "Tell you what, I'd like to have a personal discussion with that gracious lady. For the good of Looziana."

"My mother is in Spain."

"I think I could make Miz Sinclair see my position on this here issue. When your mama comes back, maybe she'll do me the honor of havin' dinner with me."

"She has no immediate plans to return."

"Keep me posted, though. Hunh?"

As the Cajuns say, "*Il a le nez dur*"—a hardnose.

Crowley, having made it all the way from a tenant farmer's shack to the governor's mansion, perceives no limit to his prospects. Actually, there's a better chance that Lady Di's next baby will be Mr. T's than this coon ass has of ever breaking bread with my mother, but I wouldn't tell him so.

Clementine Vigé Sinclair is no snob, but she has a strong sense of what is appropriate.

There came a dainty tapping on the door, and Gervis hopped to admit a corn-fed young thing wearing a Tulane Green Wave T-shirt and not much else.

His Excellency rose to greet the coed with surging enthusiasm and waved her off to the bedroom.

He winked at me. "I got to confer wit' one of my constituents. I'm sure you understand."

"That girl wasn't even old enough to vote last election."

"I'll run again." With that he turned, zipped into the room after her, and closed the door.

The hell of it is that he will run, too. And he'll win again. And I'll have to vote for him again because in the whole state of Louisiana no one will be able to find a candidate who's any better.

Gervis, in his role as his brother's factotum, then sought to lighten the mood. He told me the story about a Cajun woman, Mrs. Boudreaux, who sent her boy Clovis off to college in Lafayette.

"So after he come back from college, this boy Clovis, he 'thinks himself' see. He ain't even a coonass no more. And he went and forgot all his French. He's so goddamn educated he only speaks English now."

"I know some like that."

"So he's goin' round the garden, sayin', 'Mama? What you call this in French? Tell me what's the French word for rake?' "And the mama, she's workin' there in the garden sayin', 'Mais, the more I send that to college, the stupider it gets, yeah.'

"Next thing you know this college boy, he goes step on this self-same rake he don't know the name for. And it bounces right up and hits him in the face. So then he hollers out, 'Maudit fils putain de rateau m'a pete ca sur le nez!'

It was a good joke and I laughed.

Stepping out of the elevator on the lobby floor, I almost collided with a black raincoated figure who was rushing in. We were nose to nose for a milli-second, then he drew back in surprise as though he knew me. I am happy to say he did not, for this person represented a particularly greasy ethnic type, with dark vulture-like features. I was minded of that hapless Arabian who bumped into Death in a Bagdad marketplace and, scared out of his wits, borrowed a horse and rode like mad to Samarra to escape him. I maneuvered around the man and turned right through the lobby.

It was nearly five and nearly dark as I left the hotel. There was a slight drizzle out of Bourbon and day tourists were clustered in doorways and under the awnings of strip clubs. As I turned up my collar and headed toward Esplanade, a cheery looking woman with a mid-Western accent caterwauled, "You don't come in outa the rain?"

I smiled back at her. "What rain?"

In this humid sub-tropical climate we have our own idea of precipitation. Basic criteria: If your underwear is still dry, you are not "in the rain." When your car is floating, it's a wee bit damp out.

Once on Esplanade, I didn't turn toward the house but continued up Chartres instead to sort my thoughts. By now the light shower had abated and the sun, veiled by the gray sky, had gone down behind me. Stoop-sitters had long retreated indoors and I had the street to myself, hearing nothing but draining gutters and my own footsteps.

Passing Elysian Fields, I came on an old pickup truck, its lights still burning, parked in front of a run-down, green-painted double. I moved to the front door without ascending its three brick stairs and knocked on the panel.

After some internal mumbling and footsteps, the door was scraped open by the householder, a black man in t-shirt and paint-spattered work pants, with beer in hand.

I pointed. "You left your truck lights on."

"Geez, man. Thanks! That battery ain't no good anyhow and I sure woulda had to jump it." Then he squinted past my shoulder. "Who that dude be?"

I turned to look where he looked but saw no one.

"Where?"

"Gone now. White dude. Looked funny, that's all."

As he ducked back inside to fetch his keys, I continued along Chartres to work up an appetite for dinner. Robin was cooking tonight, so I'd have to be ravenous.

A dark late-model Lincoln Continental nosed along down the block at four miles an hour as though in no particular hurry to get anywhere but I paid it no attention. There are a lot of drivers like that in Louisiana.

We New Orleanians systematically practice defensive walking, turning to check the terrain every thirty feet, and crossing mid-block and crossing again to avoid suspicious-looking night strollers. So I was alerted to the movement of the man coming up behind me.

He didn't look like your standard-grade local mugger because he was white, middle-aged, and graceless in a black raincoat. But he was walking faster than seemed natural for him, as though to overtake me, at the same time twisting his head to look in every direction but mine. Being a typically suspicious city dude, I quickened my pace to get out of his range. My heart beat faster when he sped up behind me and so, coincidentally did the Lincoln. Then in the same minute I saw another man, similarly attired, stride toward me from the opposite direction. I stopped short when I realized that this second man was the very one I had encountered outside the elevator back at the hotel.

And I again recalled the Arabian tale and Death's ominous final line.

"I was startled to see the man here in Bagdad. For tonight I have an appointment with him. In Samarra."

Impelled by a rush of adrenalin I bolted and, dodging behind the Lincoln, tore off across Chartres to vault over a four foot iron fence on the other side. And I never looked back or stopped running until I reached the corner of Royal and Frenchman. There, leaning against a lamp post and panting like a dog, I paused for a long look around and satisfied myself that the pursuers were nowhere in sight. If pursuers they had been.

If the men had stalked me with robbery in mind, they were bungling oafs. I never carry enough cash to make a payday for one mugger let alone a team.

I ruminated over their motive during my walk back to Esplanade. But as the street lights blinked on overhead, I had thought it all out and came to the one inevitable conclusion: I was a screaming paranoic. The driver of the Lincoln was only poking along looking for an address. And of course the black-coated men weren't chasing me at all but were only hurrying to meet each other. The one behind had sped up because he had just seen his friend in front of me. If the second man had indeed been the one I'd met back at the hotel, it was coincidence. It had to be.

They must have been flabbergasted when I reacted like a crazy and took off.

By the time I reached the house I had all but forgotten the incident.

Chapter Four
Tuesay Morning, March 7

I should have been checking bills of lading.

But instead, I was shirking, just cocked back in the swivel chair behind my desk, ruminating about one Brad Rutledge. Why had I met him at the corner of Royal and Dumaine, and what paper had he waved in my face? His last wave as it turned out. Why had it made me so angry? Enough to strangle the man, according to Les Borden. Would I strangle a good tenant who paid his rent on time, in any case? And if I did, would I then hang him up in the closet? For what? To dry? It was all too confusing.

My office TV was tuned to E.S.N. and I was distracted by a horse jumping Grand Prix until the station break. Then the first commercial got me wondering why Dick Van Patten's three grown sons ride around in the back seat of his Oldsmobile instead of having cars of their own, not to say homes and families of their own. I had just decided that Van Patten must be a very strict father indeed when Steve Hicks knocked on the open door.

"Hey, Matt. Did that guy ever catch up with you yesterday?"

My feet slid off the desk as I jolted upright. "Which guy?"

"Some weird looking dude in a black raincoat. Came in about four and asked where he could find my boss. Naturally, I bragged on you."

"Bragged?"

"Told him you were in consultation with our venerable Governor over at the Royal Sonesta. He was real impressed."

"I see. Well, he didn't quite catch up to me."

"He'll probably be back."

"I'll bet."

So those men had been following me after all. And with no good in mind, or they wouldn't have chosen a dark street for the meeting. But what for? I couldn't believe it was robbery. Did they have anything to do with Brad?

And as Steve surmised, they would be back.

He clapped for my attention. "Say, you know who just walked in? The Cowboy himself."

"Really? Not buying furniture for his stable, I presume."

"Should I show him back here?"

"With all appropriate obsequies."

And I sprang up to welcome the great man as he brushed both door jambs on his way in.

Charles "Cowboy" Eisenhardt is only six feet three. I say "only" because he gives an impression of physical power and hugeness far greater than his actual bulk.

"Howdy, Matt." He adjusted his glasses downward and studied me through the thick lenses. (His eyes are the only weak thing about him.) "The cops said maybe you can help me with somethin'."

"I hope I can, Cowboy."

He tipped off his ever present ten-gallon Stetson with its bedraggled red feather in the band. This rustic headgear lends him a comical aspect when he wants, or a fearsome one when he wants. Whatever he wants.

"I got to ask you about Brad Rutledge."

"I can't help too much there. Say, you're limping."

"Dern right, I am." He turned around and lifted a trouser leg. A large bruise of purple-going-green discolored his right calf. "And I got another one jes' like it on t'other side."

"Fight with a woman?"

"Not that fierce. Was jes' that goldarn grizzly I'm puttin' up fer the zoo."

"I saw a picture of your bear in yesterday's paper. They were shooting him with tranquilizers."

"That was just to move the good ol' boy. He sure was feelin' ornery when he woke up this mornin'." Cowboy rubbed at the bruise. "An' he was only playin'. Sure hate to have 'im mad at me. That there's the only critter in Looziana who's badder 'n I am."

He patted the cigarettes in his shirt pocket and glanced around for an ashtray. I quickly produced a Steuben glass candy dish and held it out to him like an offering to a malevolent god.

Eisenhardt didn't know that I was breaking my hard rule of no smoking on the premises for him alone. And he couldn't have guessed why.

I remember it was the spring of 1965 when I was into my Carnaby Street period, wearing my hair long as the good brothers at Jesuit would tolerate. Each day after class I'd climb out of my uniform and into the counter-culture costume of striped bells and a flowered body shirt. I was convinced that I looked like Donovan during that era, but realistically I probably came closer to Twiggy.

One evening late in May I had just passed my Latin final and was a proud high school senior, sashaying down St. Ann Street to show off my "Mersey look." But I walked too far for a boy alone at that time of night. I had passed South Rampart and was all the way up to the graveyard before I came in touch with my own mortality. Three bikers appeared suddenly, like chain-swinging images out of a horror film.

"What we got here? A little ol' queer for dinner," said the largest billy goat gruff. His eyes were bright with uppers.

The short one, also chemically propelled, bounced and shouted, "This our turf! Death to invaders!"

The middle-sized one was a doer. He swung his bike

chain around his head to test its weight, then moved at me.

"Ain't beat up a hippy in a whole week. Ah'm gonna do this one good!"

I slowly backed away from them till I hit the stone wall of the cemetery. Unless I could back through it, there was no escaping whatever fate they had in mind for me. Pleading would only enhance their sport, and an old-fashioned girlish scream would bring not rescuers, but a few more like them.

That's when *he* descended on the scene like a buckskin-clad guardian angel. Charles Eisenhardt was just limbering up with a stroll back from the Fairgrounds, where he had been taking most of the prize money in the Gulf South Circuit Rodeo.

The man was magnificent in his "good guy" Western garb, with fringed jacket, turquoise-clipped string tie, and a grand gold and sterling Rodeo Champion belt buckle.

I remember his eyes glinting dangerously behind those same thick glasses. I'd read about him in the sports section, but this was my first actual sight of the Cowboy.

"Y'all got intolerable bad manners."

His voice was quiet, as befitted one used to being obeyed.

But the three belligerents were so spaced-out that they didn't recognize absolute power when they saw it. The shortest of them, presuming himself covered by his comrades, advanced, chortling and swinging his chain.

Cowboy easily caught the chain in his left hand, then moved in on the man and picked him up by his armpits, shaking him experimentally.

"You're too small."

And he threw him farther than I can throw a cat.

The other two rushed Cowboy in a pincer blitz movement. He coolly grabbed each by the leather collar and smashed their faces together, which made them lose all interest in the puny hippy with the flowered shirt.

While they were still sobbing and bleeding and crawling away, my savior turned to me. The rising moon reflected off his steel-rimmed eyeglasses.

"Fairies oughta stay in after dark."

Now, twenty years later, there was no way he could associate me with that misguided flower child. But it was worth enduring the smoke from his Marlboro now wafting around my office ceiling fan.

My largest fauteuil groaned under the Cowboy's two hundred and fifty pounds, and he overloaded the ottoman with his ostrich–skin booted feet, dropping his Stetson over one knee.The big man looked like he couldn't be moved with a winch, but I'd once seen him spring from that same position and kick two men in the chin within five seconds.

That happened while we were sharing a pitcher of Carta Blanca Beer in a Decatur Street bar back in '79. The issue had been an insult to a lady, and she wasn't even his lady. (She wasn't even a lady.)

"Matt, they tol' me you was the last to see poor Brad alive."

"Second to last."

"Um." He nodded at the ceiling. "Yup. See I had an appointment to meet him up on the Moon Walk at two o'clock. When he never showed, I didn't know he'd got himself hanged. So I just sat there and looked at the dern river all by my lonesome till four in the evenin'. Stood up like an ugly girl."

"I'm sorry."

"The feller had his eye on some of my property, and we were set to do some serious horse tradin'."

"I never thought you would sell any of that land. St. Tammany Parish is hot now."

"Yeah, but I can't hold onto it all. Got a chance to expand my operation and I need some serious money." I tried not to wince when he flicked an ash. "I done signed a ninety-day option for that hombre. Now I got to know if his partner's got it or what."

"That's worth thinking about. Apparently Brad had some essential document with him when he spoke to me."

"Was it my option?"

"I couldn't tell you. I had an epileptic seizure right after our meeting and forgot that I even saw him yesterday.

He looked alarmed. "You're given to fits?"

"It's not exactly demonic possession, Cowboy. Some years ago I cracked my head, and I still get these spells."

"That's too bad. But you might could remember your meetin' with Brad again."

"Some of it. But probably not enough to help track down your option, assuming that was the paper in question."

"Sure would like to get hold of that sucker. Whoever's got it can turn himself a good profit."

"You're already making the best use of your land that I can see. How are the horses?"

"All sleek and showy. The only way I keep 'em." He talked around his cigarette. "Say, Matt, why don't you come over to my place tomorrow and try out my new course. You can have your pick of mounts."

"That's a strong temptation. I haven't ridden anything but this chair in months. Maybe I'd better get back up before my thighs turn to mush."

" 'Long about three o'clock then? I know Jessica would like to see you."

"I would like to see her, too. Thank you, I'm looking forward to it."

The office door was still open so my fellow committee member Edwina Devon sailed through it unannounced, carrying a folder of ads, bills, and statistics.

"Hello, Matty. Did I come at a bad time?"

"Never. You're always welcome and wanted, dear."

Edwina is one of my own people. The Devons have

been in New Orleans nearly as long as the Sinclairs. Also, she is as finely bred as a Glencoe filly herself, slender and petite with large blue eyes and long, dark wavy hair, caught now in a Gibson Girl upsweep.

"Flatterer." She dumped her papers on my desk then whirled around. "Oh hi, Cowboy! I didn't expect to see you here."

And I didn't expect to see her kiss him either, but she undertook to do exactly that, standing on her dainty little toes. As she still didn't reach his mouth, he picked her up and lifted her the rest of the way.

"Hi, sweet stuff. Your boyfriend Bill Oakes will be out to my place this afternoon."

"Yes, I want him to try Cricket."

"Cricket?" The echo was me.

"The Eisenhardts are boarding her for me," Edwina said. "And my other jumper, Tam."

"I thought you kept your horses at Audubon Park."

"Their track gets too muddy after a hard rain. Cowboy has a raised gravel bridle path you can ride all year, and he's nearly finished a new steeplechase course that's absolutely thrilling!

"Yup." He bobbed his head. "All set up permanent. I just invited Matt to try the course tomorrow."

"Why don't you come too?" I asked. "Pace me."

She started to unfurl a smile but it collapsed midway.

"No, I can't. Tomorrow I have that tiresome old trustees' meeting. Anyhow, you be sure to put him on Cricket. You know my bay jumper, Matty."

"I used to take her out when you were abroad. Cricket and I are great friends."

"Okey-douake. I'll have the bay saddled and waiting." Eisenhardt bent to give Edwina a farewell kiss on the top of her head then waved his hat and swaggered off into the sunset like Matt Dillon.

She finally kissed the proper person, myself, then got comfortable on the settee, crossing her legs and allowing one of her Bass Weejuns to dangle provocatively.

"You know where I first met Cowboy?"

"No. And please don't ever tell me."

Edwina Devon was the wildest girl in our crowd back during the hippy era. The good Sisters of the Sacred Heart could never make a regulation convent girl out of her; she put in more time out on suspension than in her classrooms at the Academy. And her vacations were spent exploring the murky demimonde of non-Catholics in Decatur Street dives.

Edwina was only sixteen years old that sweltering June when she thought it might be "a groove" to go slumming down in Bertie's, the hangout of the Galloping Goose bikers' club. Sometime that summer she gave up her virginity to a particularly repulsive cretin called Snake in the ingenuous conviction that her love and devotion would turn him into a noble citizen.

When she missed her period the next month, Snake was pleased at the prospect of a little "rug rat" on the way, since it proved his virility. And he didn't intend to support the child anyhow. But by then Edwina had recovered her senses to the point of remembering who she was and that unwed motherhood wasn't in the Devon tradition.

At first she resorted to a fistful of Humprey's Elevens. When those weren't effective, there came a bout of fasting, followed by hours of calisthenics and attempts to lift her mother's chinoiserie breakfront. I was her last resort.

I was nineteen that summer and making good checks off-shore, so the money was no problem. I carried her straight to Doc Knight, the only expert abortionist on the Delta back before abortion was legal. I recall that there was an issue of *Time* magazine in the waiting room. I read up on the Six-Day War and the Israeli forces' capture of Jerusalem while the doc earned his $150 fee on the other side of the wall.

Afterward I took Edwina out for an Orange Julius, she being too young to drink.

Two months later, I had the honor of the first dance at her debut at the Roosevelt Hotel. And she was slim and lovely in her white taffeta ball gown.

Edwina seems more tame now but hasn't yet lost her delightfully devilish vivacity. And these days she was devoting her time and irrepressible energy to a most worthy effort, the defeat of the casino bill.

"I had to leave a whole·bundle of statistical data at home. There was simply too much to lug over here. But you should put your lawyer's eye on it anyway."

"I don't mind stopping by your house to check it out. I have to see Lieutenant Washington at four, but after that I'm through for the day."

"Frank? What are you going to see him for?"

"I'm a murder suspect."

"Oh, Matty. You're kidding!" But her sparkling eyes said she hoped I wasn't.

"I may be kidding, but Frank was serious when he asked me to meet him at Brennan's."

When I arrived at the restaurant on Royal Street, I was exactly on time for our appointment, but Frank wasn't. So I walked out to the bricked courtyard, took one of the iron chairs within splashing distance of the fountain, and ordered my first Sazerac of the day. I was sipping it slowly and reading last week's *Barron's* when a firm had squeezed my shoulder.

"Matty, buy me a drink?" A voice I'd heard before.

I looked up into hypnotic green eyes and a handsome sculpted face framed by blue-black wavy hair, all crowning a lithe young physique cald in soft gray cashmere.

"Lawrence Dale." Then I remembered that the punk's original name was something Italian. "Or what are you calling yourself these days?"

"Lawrence is good enough. Mind if I sit down?"

"You will anyway. Attempted murder carries some heavy time. Why aren't you in prison where you belong?"

"I'm appealing."

"You certainly are."

Lawrence Dale must be twenty-five now but he looks like an undergraduate, an Ivy Leaguer in his Oxford suit with the just-back-in-fashion flared trousers—a style his kind would be sure to seize upon.

Mob money had financed the boy's New England prep school education. For years he was carefully polished, just like a gun. Lawrence's elocution is crisp, with a bit of Boston and some Yale, while his aplomb is studiedly languorous. This "lazy rich kid" persona is ideal camouflage for a cold-blooded hitman whose idea of postcoital play is a lethal hypodermic.

He took the chair opposite and leaned back, crossing right ankle over left knee to show the clocks on his stockings.

"Guess what? That judge didn't like homosexuals."

"Who does?"

"We found a twenty-year-old newspaper quote in which he likened our kind to 'animals and deviates.' I'm deeply wounded. Aren't you?"

"No."

"Such a publicly avowed bigot should have recused himself. At least that's why my lawyers are being paid an awful lot of money to argue."

"Considering that the victim, my unhappy self, was just a gay as the perpetrator, I don't see how your argument will hold up."

"Gee, I hope there are no hard feelings about that, Matty."

"No, indeed not. Some of my best friends try to murder me. Hardly worth a grudge."

He flicked away the thought with a particle of lint.

"That was business. Anyhow, after we'd made such beautiful love together, I felt sure you'd rather *I* take the ten thousand than some stranger." He called Sid, the waiter, over with one imperious finger. "I'll have a cherry cola, please. And bring another for my friend."

Sid either knew or sensed that Lawrence was more than he appeared to be, because he moved on this order faster than I'd ever seen him move before.

I watched Sid sprint to the outside bar then turned back to the punk. "You seem none the worse for your visit upstate."

A dainty sigh. "Angola isn't too rough for someone both rich and beautiful. You know, I had those black brutes dueling over me. With cane knives."

"What are you doing back in New Orleans? More business?"

"Not about you, love. You know that contract was withdrawn after Manguno died." His smile would melt a heart colder than mine. "Not about anyone."

"So why did you order a pop? As though staying sober to keep your gun arm steady."

"I never drink. I simply can't afford even ten minutes of diminished capacity. As for the gun ..." He opened his coat to show there was no holster.

I said, "It's strapped above your left ankle."

He laughed and didn't deny it. "Anyway, I want you to know that we're both on the same side."

"Side of what?"

"The concern I'm working for doesn't want gambling in New Orleans either."

"Um ... Let me guess. The Baptist Church? No, that couldn't be it. How about Gamblers Anonymous?" I clinked my ice in the rocks glass. "No, I don't think that's the bunch either. Try again. Just maybe some mob forces in Nevada and Atlantic City who would rather not share the action. Am I getting warm?"

"I don't drop names, love."

Sid reappeared with our drinks in double time, and Lawrence drank his pop elegantly, in small sips, before resuming.

"The people I represent will pay you one hundred and fifty percent of assessed value for your riverfront property."

"And do what with it?"

"Build it up, burn it down. What do you care?"

"I care. See, I don't trust you much, babyface. Incidentally, did you kill Brad Rutledge?" He smiled and dimples appeared in both cheeks. Lawrence was still a beautiful little piece in spite of all he'd been and done. A real-life Dorian Grey.

"He was what? Left hanging in a closet?"

"I hear it was quite disgusting."

"Does that sound like a professional job to you? I work neat. No struggle, no blood."

"I know you do. But some of your fellow buttonmen may be less tidy."

"If so, they wouldn't stay in business long. You have my word that no one in my organization killed Brad Rutledge. Now, will you sell us the acreage?"

"Sorry. I really can't."

"Be a smart guy, Matty. You can take the money and buy something of equal value. Get everyone off your neck."

"You know I would."

"You would?"

"But for one invariable variable. My mother."

"The lady gave you autonomy over all her real estate holdings. She must trust your judgment."

"Theoretically. She trusts me to do exactly as she wishes. And mother does not wish to sell land."

"Never?"

"Never as long as she has lived. Her moto is 'I'm not trying to buy all the land in the world. I just want the piece next to mine.'" I tried the second Sazerac. It had been mixed with a better bourbon. "Mother buys land, holds it, rents it out, pays taxes on it . . . She will do anything a person can do with land except sell it."

The delectable little murderer wiped condensation off his glass. "In short, your mother would rather call all the forces of hell down on you than sell us the property."

"That would be her feeling."

Lawrence narrowed his eyes. "Maybe you can't move on this. Tell you what, though. So long as the Sinclairs own that property, my people are content. Our position is covered for nothing. But please contact me before you sell it to anyone else. My friends will top any legitimate offer."

He held up an engraved business card with a Trade Mart address. Then he rose, slipped it into my coat pocket, and kissed my cheek. "It's all right, love. Italian men always kiss in public."

"But I'm not Italian."

"I'll get the check on the way out."

He winked a good-bye and glided across the courtyard toward Lieutenant Frank Washington, who was just walking in. Dale caught his eye and bowed.

Frank passed him without seeming to notice and joined me, taking the chair Lawrence had vacated.

"Did you see who's in town?" I asked.

"I know, Matt."

"Why didn't you bust him? You know he's dirty."

"Yeah, strapped to his left leg. But remember what happened the last time we picked Dale up for carrying a weapon?"

"I was there."

"I mean in court. Little Lord Fauntleroy just blubbered to the jury that he needed protection because some beast had raped him. We couldn't introduce his record, so they cut him loose." Sid brought him a domestic beer on a tray. "It would have been easier to convict Shirley Temple in the Lindbergh case."

"He won't be young and cute forever."

"People in his line of work are ephemeral anyhow. But the kid might be useful to us now." Frank leaned back and flexed his flat feet. "For once you and he are on the same side."

"That's what he said."

"Dale works for the Sacci family out of Vegas. They

already got their feelings hurt by the new gambling resorts in Atlantic City. East Coast high rollers are staying closer to home. Now they're afraid of losing the southern action, too."

"And if our governor ever stops flying up there, the casinos will have to lay off a hundred croupiers."

"Right now we've got plenty of bad actors in town pushing *for* the casino and pushing hard. So why not balance the ecology? I'll just let precious Lawrence Dale run around here pushing back. He's deadlier than all of them. In fact, I was the one who told him you would be here so he could drop by and say hi."

"You're a real matchmaker, Frank. Who are you going to fix me up with next? Charles Manson?"

"Don't underestimate me, friend. The way I've figured it, that little punk contract killer is going to be your guardian angel."

Chapter 5
Tuesay Evening, March 7th

Edwina Devon lives by herself in the re-gentrifying Bywater district of New Orleans. She had left her iron cornstalk gate ajar for me; I stopped to lock it before walking up the broad front steps and across the tiled porch of her raised Victorian.

I didn't need to ring the bell because she was already waiting on the other side of her leaded-glass double doors.

She took my hand. "You're right on time. I love that."

"I didn't give you a time."

"You're right in season then." She led me through the narrow foyer which was decorated with a Chinese tapestry. "I just got in myself, Matty. I was shopping for spring water."

"I hope you got the right size."

When we hit the living room, I had the feeling of walking onto the set of a romantic farce. All the accoutrements of an assignation were there: bowls of flowers on every table, heaps of freshly fluffed pillows, even the fragrance of Shalimar coming out of nowhere from everywhere.

Edwina had been my ideal woman for about fifteen years, and I would have been thrilled to make love to her at any time. So if she returned my interest at last, I would be completely at her disposal, although needing no pillows, perfume, or the ambiance of an Eastern harem. Just Edwina and I all alone in the universe, floating free, would have been my idea of nirvana.

But like most women, Edwina had a fantasy percep-
tion of the mating act, colored by films and romantic
novels. If she had only guessed how very much I wanted
her, she would have fled in a panic. So I made an
effort to stay cool and act whatever role was expected
of me.

"Gee, nice flowers."

"Thank you." She waved to the coffee table. "There
are all those photocopies. They're vitally important, so
I think you'd better study them."

"I certainly will."

"Now, if you'll excuse me," she said casually. "I'm
just going to get out of these hot clothes." And I was
left alone with the vitally important papers as she made
for the bedroom.

I cased her stereo system, tuned the FM to JOY 102
for mood music, then settled on the couch to save her
the trouble of finagling me over there.

When Edwina reappeared five minutes later, she was
wearing only a simple cotton shift and her pantyhose
had been removed. Fortunately. There is no graceful
way to pull those things off, even when the woman
helps.

I had spread her notes on the coffee table and was
doing my stuffy lawyer bit. "I've considered all options,
Edwina, and I think what's going to pull this through
are cold, hard statistics. No one can vote for gambling
once they understand what happened in Atlantic City."

"No, they can't," she conceded seriously. "That's why
we took out the ad in the *Times-Picayune*. To tell our
side of it. Would you like something to drink?"

"Hmm. Whatever you're having."

What she was having was Madeira in a crystal goblet.
I sipped at mine then smiled as though I were being
slowly warmed up.

"Just for fun," I asked, "how much did the ad cost
us?"

"Not fun at all. The space alone was seven-thousand

four hundred and thirteen dollars . . . and sixty-nine cents."

"For a nonprofit outfit on a weekday?"

"We took a full page. By the way, the committee's only got six thousand in our campaign chest. Who's going to pay the balance?"

"It looks like I am, if you can't find another patsy."

"It's not your responsibility. We'll raise the money somehow." And she sat close beside me, draping her arm around my neck and rubbing it sensuously.

"You're very uptight, Matty. You ought to relax a little."

"You're right," cool, dispassionate visitor admitted morosely. "I've been taking end-of-season inventory at the shop and then throwing myself into this committee work. Sorry. I must be dull company."

She plumped a pillow behind my back. "But you're not. I love being with you."

"Thank you, Edwina. You're a warm, understanding lady."

She moved in kissing-close to me and I met her lips hesitantly, as though I couldn't avoid it, then at the invitation, her tongue. When her breath quickened, I cupped her breasts under her shift. They were perfect—a Frenchman's idea of perfect. They would fit exactly in champagne glasses.

I caressed her nipples in circular motions while nuzzling the pulse point beneath her ear.

"Beautiful . . . ? Do you understand what you're doing?"

I felt her little breasts swell under my hands.

She assured me with kisses as she unbuttoned my shirt and ran thin, delicate hands over my shoulders.

"I've wanted this for a long time."

"Not half as long."

I sensed that it was time to take charge, so picked her up in my arms and carried her through the hall to the bedroom, stopping for deep kisses along the way.

Edwina weighed no more than one hundred and ten, so I, being fairly strong, was able to whip aside the covers and lay her down without any awkwardness. Making love to a woman involves much intricate choreography, and any break in the flow can destroy her mood.

Before joining her on the bed, I reached for my wallet and shook out the Trojan. Her body stiffened at this intrusive gesture to common sense.

"It's all right, Matty. I'm protected."

"But I'm not. And I don't want to get pregnant either."

After I had plied all the lover's arts and assured myself that she was satisfied, I fell back on the pillow two seconds away from sleep. She pressed against me, her warm breath stirring my chest hair.

"You're a fine erotic technician."

"Thank you, ma'am. I give it my best."

"Matty? How long have we known each other?"

I suppressed a groan. After any act of intercourse, my blood pressure tends to plunge so low that I'm legally dead in most states. If this relationship were to continue, she must be made to respect my postcoital somnolence. But for now, as the lady wanted meaningful conversation, I was forced to oblige or be thought a cad.

I gathered her in my arms. "I remember the first time I saw you. Mother made me hold you on my lap while she poured tea for your Aunt Loretta. I think it was late summer, because the crepe myrtle was blooming in the back garden and the fuchsia flowers kept dropping onto your brand-new pink-striped sunsuit. You would pick them up in your chubby little hands and say 'Pwitty!' "

" 'Pwitty'?" Edwina laughed and burrowed into my shoulder. "I was three years old when I got that sunsuit. And you were six. The closest I ever had to a big brother. How come we never made love before?"

"I was always willing. Maybe you would have felt incestuous."

"A few years ago, but not now. We started out as brother and sister and grew up into two people who have an awful lot in common. Don't you think?"

I put both hands up to cover a yawn. "No argument."

"So let's not let go of this, all right? I mean let's . . . sort of 'go steady.' "

"But, darling. I thought you were 'sort of going steady' already."

"You mean with Brad? Oh, I met him in connection with this committee work, but we only dated a couple of times."

"I didn't know that."

"The man was ill-mannered and had no idea how to treat a woman. So naturally I switched over to his partner, Bill Oakes."

"Naturally."

"She hoisted herself up on my solar plexus.

"Hey, I'll bet a *woman* killed poor Brad."

"Because he was ill-mannered?"

"He wouldn't even open a car door, for goodness sake."

"No female could have killed him, though, even for such an important reason as that. Only a man would have been strong enough to lift a hundred and forty—pound dead weight and hang him in the closet. . . . Tell me about you and Bill."

"Oh, we've been dating casually." A shrug of bare shoulders. "He told me he likes riding, too. But aside from that, we have nothing in common."

"I've seen Oakes on Bum Phillip's show. He's handsome as the very devil and stands to make millions with that development syndicate. Your boy is a good prospect."

"In his way, I suppose. The silly man begs me to marry him; he even carries the ring around with him. But Bill has no breeding, Matty. He'd only known me fifteen minutes before he told me I had beautiful legs."

"How crass." I was fighting a yawn. "He should have looked at your legs and told you you had beautiful *eyes*."

"Yes, but he doesn't know any better. Why he actually sits and watches Woody Woodpecker cartoons on television."

"No culture." My voice was fading. "I'm a Tom and Jerry man myself."

"It gets worse. In bed he's strictly a clod. I suppose he's trying, poor thing. But he just doesn't have your skill."

"Maybe he gets too involved. Why don't you just be patient and show him what you want?"

"That's so tiresome, though." She rubbed my shoulders. "It should be instinctive, don't you think? Anyhow, you and I are so compatible; let's not waste it."

I kissed her hair. "Let's not belabor the obvious either. Or are you forgetting that I'm gay?"

Her eyes crinkled. "Your 'thing' looked pretty straight a while ago."

Finally she gave me leave to fall asleep.

When I woke up, some twenty minutes later, it was with a throbbing headache and a sense of disorientation. There were some moments before I realized that I was in Edwina's house and that it was her cool hand on my brow.

"Are you all right, Matty? You had a seizure."

Damn! Again damn!

"Are you sure that was it?"

"Well, you were making this low animal sound and flailing your arms and legs and foaming at the mouth."

"That was it. Sorry." I tried to roll out of bed and failed.

"Say"—she bit a knuckle—"it's awfully mean to bring this up right now . . . but is it hereditary?"

"What?" My mind was trying to reglue itself. "The epilepsy? No. I took a fall when I was a kid."

"Oh, good!" She clapped her hands then quickly put them over her mouth in self-censure. "I'm sorry. I only meant good that your children won't get it."

"Anyone might get it. But it's not contagious. Toss me my pants."

By seven o'clock, I had made it back home to Esplanade Avenue. I stepped through the front door and dropped my coat on the hall table.

"Robin? I smell smoke!"

Apparently my angry tone roused him from a sullen torpor. He rolled off the living room couch and put his little nose up for a sniff. "Nothing's burning. Oh, you mean the cigarette smoke."

"And I mean, where did it come from?"

"Not me, Matty. You know I never fool with tobacco. Ask Sigrid; she's still back there."

The accused ventured out of the kitchen now, holding a dish towel as though she had been gainfully employed, but it was dry and still folded. And she looked guilty as hell.

I assumed my sternest aspect.

"When you took this job, you told me you didn't smoke!"

"I didn't, Mister Matt. I mean, I don't. Truly, But it was jes' sperimentin', you know? I mean only this one time. I jes' foun' this cigarette on the street an' I thought I'd try it. But I jes' lit it once't and put it out ag'in." Sigrid had lied to me many times before and, as usual, her explanation was so convoluted and brainless that it would take an acrostics expert to make any sense of it. "I hates it, though," she bubbled on. "It didn't mean nothin'. Please don' git mad."

"I will not have smoking in my house, Sigrid!"

"Yes sir, Mister Matt. I mean, no sir. No smokin'. I swear I won' do it no more." And she backed into the kitchen, away from my righteous wrath.

Robin said, "You wouldn't have hired her if you'd known she was a smoker."

"Right."

"Are you going to fire her?"

"No. That is, not yet."

"I'm glad you're giving her another chance," he said. "It's not her fault she had to grow up in an uncivilized racist part of the country."

"I beg your pardon?"

I shouldn't have asked, because that only propelled him into yet more West Coast liberal jargon from that sunny region where everyone seems to be noble, Christ-like, and middle class.

"You can't help being a southerner and that your ancestors brought Sigrid's ancestors here in chains. But at least you're trying to make up for three hundred years of oppression with this job. How else is she going to break out of the welfare-poverty cycle?"

"She's not. But there is one glimmer of hope. I notice she's stayed late to finish her work in the kitchen."

"Actually, she came late. I had to wait around till two o'clock to let her in. Then I went to the sale at Brooks Brothers, but I was back by five to supervise her"

"Supervise? A good foreman doesn't work supine."

"As foreman. I recommend that you fire Blanche. She scratched up the back door something awful."

"We just painted that!" I bolted through the kitchen, where Sigrid was now washing dishes harder than she had ever washed anything in her life. Maybe even using soap.

I pushed open the screen door to the courtyard to observe the damage. The screening had been slashed to ribbons, and their were deep grooves in the week-old coat of paint. It appeared that Blanche had been filing her nails on the back door for a good hour.

"Blanche! Where are you?"

Our resident Boxer heard the extreme displeasure in my tone and came slinking into the kitchen, belly so low that she might have won a limbo contest. I pointed to the evidence.

"Did you do that?"

She put her square head down and groveled miserably until I realized I was chewing out the wrong bitch. I turned and addressed the real culprit.

"Sigrid? Why was Blanche left in the yard so long?"

"Well, I jes' went to the sto', Mister Matt. You needed me to make groceries an' that dog was sleepin' outside real peaceful, so I lef' her there. Didn't think it would do no harm. Sho' didn't."

"No harm? Blanche is a *watchdog*. She can't do her job if she's locked outside."

"I'm truly sorry."

"A team of burglars might have been in here taking the place apart, and all Blanche could do about it is . . ."

Scratch on the back door.

I took a fast inventory of all the rooms—TV, stereo, cash on hand . . . Nothing seemed to be missing. Professional burglars wouldn't have bothered to be neat. As for the most likely amateur, I didn't kid myself that Sigrid was too honest to steal, but she would have wanted some assurance that she could get away with it. And I knew where she, her mother, and her six children stayed.

A loud and frantic barking interrupted my dark speculations. Blanche was scrambling around in the foyer, beside herself with rage that a black man had stopped at the front gate.

Lewis Wofford didn't need to announce himself with the doorbell. His barely portable radio was playing a Janet Jackson record loud enough to break windows.

"Sigrid, your ride is here," Robin called, unnecessarily.

She was out of the kitchen in a second, pulling on her fake fox coat. "I be back on Monday, Mister Matt."

"We're looking forward to it." I opened the front door and watched her scurry down the front walk to the gate, where her suitor demonstrated his ardor by switching his radio from right shoulder to left so he could take her arm.

Wofford was as skinny as Sigrid was fat, wore a green suit, and had a dip in his walk. A project dandy. That they deserved each other was the worst thing one could say about either of them.

We had no plans to go out again, so I used my chain and padlock on the gate then came back inside to rejoin Robin, who was horizontal again.

"Say, lover. Don't you greet your man with a stiff drink like any good housewife?"

He pulled himself up. "Yes, master. Right away." But he was deliberately slow in moving to the bar. "It never occurred to you that you're expected home at six fifteen? I was waiting for you since then. You didn't phone. You didn't write. I was scared something happened to you."

"I was perfectly safe at Edwina's."

"Oh yeah?" He poured the bourbon then added too much Abisante by way of subtle sabotage. The power of the powerless. "What did you do with Edwina that took up so much time?"

"We talked about committee business. Then we made love and she said she would like to go steady with me. Then I had a seizure."

He blanched. "That's terrible!"

"Second one in three days. You'd better take my pills to the pharmacy and have Sam analyze them."

"I didn't mean the *seizure* was so terrible! How could you have made love to her?"

"Just the regular way." Then I saw that he looked stricken. "Edwina is a fascinating woman. I've adored her for years."

"Oh, Matty!"

"I'm sorry, kitten. I shouldn't have told you."

"*Telling* isn't the problem. *Doing* is."

He finally finished mixing the drink and handed it over.

"That was very stupid of her to think about going steady. I hope you told her she was stupid."

"No, I told her I was hers to command."

"What!" he sputtered out and had to start up again. "She's a female!"

"That didn't escape me either. But Edwina is a very special female and wonderful company."

"It's that midlife crisis, Matty. You're going gray and you think you should straighten out with age." He poured himself a jolt of Bosco and added no more than an equal amount of milk, which is as strong as anyone can make it for oral use. I wouldn't be surprised to see him inject the stuff.

"Here I am worried again," he complained. "Why should I be worried? You've put me through this hell before."

"What are you babbling about?"

"You and these women. Every few months you get this ridiculous craving for seafood, but it never lasts more than two weeks."

"Two weeks?" I was too lazy or too proud to add more bourbon to the Sazerac and drank it as was.

"Just since I've been with you there was . . . first that secretary, Brandi. You dropped a bundle at Maison Blanche outfitting her in your favorite fall colors."

"Those were *her* favorite colors. And are you forgetting she once saved my life?"

"Then there was that fat opera star who was in town to sing with the symphony. You spent a whole week just following her around, dancing attendance like a fool."

"If you had any appreciation for coloratura, you would never say 'fat opera star.' "

"I remember when you had to pry her out of that phone booth."

"And was happy to do it. You should have heard her

'Meine Lippen Sie Kussen So Heiss.' Absolutely devastating."

"She devastated your bankbook, anyway. The antique ormolu cabinet you gave her was worth a month's profits."

"The lady came in high sharp, which was worth a lot more."

"I don't care if she whistled through her cunt." He knocked back his chocolate. "In the end, at least she went on with her tour and you came back to me. And your senses." He clasped his hands and looked at me imploringly. "I just wish I didn't have to go through this absolute misery time and again."

On this cue, I backed into the foyer. "Abracadabra, banish absolute misery!" With a conjurer's flourish, I pulled the magic white box from its hiding place beneath my coat. Robin's big brown eyes lit up as though a holiday sparkler had been ignited inside his head.

"Ooh, Matty! You brought me something! Yum!"

Put Robin in an alligator-infested swamp, on an ice floe at the Arctic Circle, or deep in hell itself. He can never be unhappy while he's eating French pastry from La Marquise.

He ran for his plate and fork while I grabbed the TV remote.

"Is there anything on?" I called from my recliner, the seat of authority.

"A fabulous film on WGN at nine. *Spartacus*!"

"I can't wait."

We watched *Spartacus* whenever it played, just to see Tony Curtis as Gaius. He was still boyish and beautiful at thirty-four, his hairless chest and outsized blue eyes giving him an air of youth and innocence. And as always there was that fatal flaw, the ear-jangling Bronx accent. Robin and I leaned forward for the full effect when the tunic-clad "Roman slave" announced his profession to Kirk Douglas as the rebel Spartacus.

"Oim a singker of sawngs."

Then we were privileged to hear Curtis's "sawng," a near-monotonal recitation rendered in New York working class dialect. The other characters in the scene all reacted as dreamily as though hearing the pure tenor trill of John McCormick in his prime.

The picture was released in 1960 and apparently wasn't thought hokey then.

After that inspiring scene, I stepped into the kitchen to smother some cabbage, but Robin called me back to the set for the denouement. When forced into gladiatorial combat, Douglas and Curtis do some third-grade fencing. Douglas gets himself outfumbled and must deliver the tragic fatal blow. So inevitably he comes to hold his dying friend in his arms. And as Curtis lies spilling his life's blood into the Roman dust, he looks up into his companion's eyes to deliver his immortal last line.

"Oy luff yoo, Spotakis."

Robin and I always laugh till we ache at that point and then turn the set off. The rest of the picture is just heterosexual drivel and anticlimactic.

Chapter 6
Wednesday Afternoon, March 8th

After lunch, I found Robin waiting outside in the Mercedes where he had passed his time playing with the radio dial, the one piece of auto equipment he operates safely and without mishap.

As I opened the right-hand door and settled into the passenger's seat, he touched an imaginary chauffeur's cap.

"Where to, boss?"

"To the Eisenhardts. You know they invited us riding."

"Horseback?"

"As opposed to what? Fishback? There's only one riding."

He turned us up North Rampart towards Elysian Fields.

"None for me, then. I'll pass. I thought you were dressed in those funny tight pants because you're into costumes."

"I don't wear these pants because I'm into costumes, but because there are no inseams to pinch."

"What about those Nazi boots?"

"To keep my feet from slipping through the stirrups."

"If you say so, okay."

"Being dragged across country by one stirrup is both embarrassing and uncomfortable."

"Okay, I said, okay."

The tourist in the car ahead stopped where there was

no stop sign, to commune with his muse. I reached over to honk him out of his reverie and we proceeded.

"Head down I-Ten toward Causeway. We're going across the lake."

"Oh boy, I've never been there."

Across the lake is St. Tammany Parish, reachable via the twenty-four-mile Lake Pontchartrain Bridge, the longest six-lane bridge in the world. The best time to pass over it is at dusk, when the western sky is darkening in layers of pink, orange, and purple. And get someone else to do the driving, because the veiw is stunning just before the sun drops.

I offered an educational commentary along the way.

"St. Tammany is the yuppie capital of Louisiana. Sort of a Marin County South."

"We have the real one," Robin averred.

"Our friend Eisenhardt bought five hundred acres of woods in the early sixties, when it was selling for beans, and hacked himself a homestead out of wilderness. Then about ten years ago, with the deterioration of the inner city—"

"You mean integration?"

I ignored that liberal jibe. "—the neighborhoods became crowded and crime-ridden. The tax base eroded. The school system went downhill—"

"Because they finally integrated the classrooms?"

"At first, we good southerners found a way around that. The year the school boards were forced to integrate by race, they started segregating by sex. They set up 'separate but equal' schools for girls and boys."

"I get it. So your daughter can't socialize with black boys."

"If I had a daughter, she would attend Sacred Heart and wouldn't socialize with any boys."

"You sound like you're seriously considering it—having a daughter.'

"I can't have anything. I've got a tipped uterus. But we digress." I watched the *poules doux* athletically paddling through the high breaking waves and counted off mile post number three. "In the late seventies, some mother got angry because the girls' school had an inferior scientific curriculum, and she sued to get her daughter into the boys' school."

" 'Separate but equal' wasn't so equal?"

"Maybe not, but it was a way of dealing with the problem. So then all the schools had to go coed again. Naturally, the middle class got disgusted and fled the city. A considerable number of them moved out this way, where the scenery is beautiful and the tap water comes fresh from a spring. And they were able to start a vital new suburban community."

"Read 'no blacks.' "

"St. Tammany has become a very fashionable area among the new would-be elite—white and black."

"But mostly—"

"Never mind."

If Robin was going to harp on about children and integration, he could talk to himself. I adjusted my seat back and watched the mile posts and the ducks until we reached Mandeville on the other end. But our destination was a good twenty miles beyond that.

The sizeable Eisenhardt place is set far into bayou country. Cowboy needs all of that acreage for his enterprise, which deals mainly with animals. He boards, trains, and shows horses and is the local expert on everything that breathes, from reptiles to primates.

His secondary enterprise is the begetting and raising of children.

Twenty years ago there wasn't even a road here, and there isn't much of one now. My driver seemed to have memorized every bump and rock on the way because he didn't miss a-one. I held onto my seat belt with both hands.

"Robin, this road is dangerous!"

"So I'm driving as fast as I can to get off it."

I momentarily regretted giving him the wheel, even

speculated that I might be able to drive more safely during a shaking, foaming seizure.

My knuckles were blue-white by the time we drove up the tree-lined private road to our destination, a rambling edifice of natural wood, stained and varnished. Eisenhardt had cleared the land and built the house and outbuildings himself. Then later, as the family grew and additions became necessary, his older sons joined the construction crew.

As we pulled up front, Missy greeted us. She's Cowboy's third and youngest wife. (And now the only legal one.) "Hi Matty!" She waved only fingers, needing both arms to hold her charge, a very long baby as pale and blond as she. Charles is out back building a corral. Just you go inside and set a spell."

"Thank you, we shall."

I'd first met Missy two years before, when she was just sixteen and fresh from some hollow tree in Kentucky. I was struck by her fragile porcelain face with those enormous eyes, bearing some resemblance to those tacky old Keene paintings.

Missy had stumbled off the Trailways bus to seek her fortune in New Orleans, with all of her worldly possessions in a brown grocery bag. Being too young to work indoors, she hit the streets that same night to sell all she had to sell—her petite and malnourished body. The girl had neither decent clothes nor street savvy, so she couldn't make more than $20 a trick. And that little bit was usually stolen from her. Certainly, she would have learned the business of survival in time—or been murdered trying—but then, for some reason, her waifish awkwardness aroused Cowboy's savior instinct and he took her into his menage.

By now Missy had learned a few social graces from her co-wives and dressed with some chic in public. But around the home grounds she still went barefoot and left her waist-length hair wild and tangled.

The front door was opened by a dark and husky

adolescent, visibly the produce of Cowboy's second wife, Carmen, a fiery, half-Indian beauty he met and married on the Mexican rodeo circuit in the early seventies. The Señora has borne him five children and become more buxom with the years, but she still retains her lusty exoticim.

The main house was tastefully decorated in different but not clashing styles and periods. A gratifying preponderance of the furniture was from New Traditions. I'd given Eisenhardt some enormous discounts through the years, although he couldn't know why.

We were directed to the ten-foot sectional in the living room, overlooking the stables and corrals. I pushed aside an issue of *Quarter Horse Journal* to make room and sat back. Through the large picture window I could see Cowboy himself carrying a tree trunk over one shoulder as easily as I would a fishing rod.

A handsome boy about six years old skipped over to the wet bar and opened up fully stocked liquor cabinet. He was red-haired, so had to be Jessica's. I accepted a bottle of pop just for form and thanked him kindly. Then I saw her. His mother.

Jessica Clouet Eisenhardt is senior wife and the only one of the three who would appeal to me personally. Even dressed in her stable clothes—jeans and blue chambray shirt—her degree of refinement was unmistakable.

I sprang up to kiss her cheek.

"So happy to see you, Jessica. This is my friend, Robin Fearing."

"How do you do, Robin." She held out a sunburned hand. "Will you be riding with us today?"

"Oh no. I'm scared of horses," Robin told her. "You can't get me up on one of those things."

"Don't mind him. The boy fell off a merry-go-round when he was three," I suggested.

Our hostess smiled. "That's all right. There's plenty to do around this place without going near the horses. . . . Tippy? Come here." The six-year-old responded with an attentiveness seldom seen in children these days. "Why don't you show Mr. Fearing some of Daddy's trophies."

"Yes, ma'am."

Robin shrugged at his dismissal and accompanied Tippy out toward the tack room adjoining the stable, where some ten years' accumulation of rodeo prizes were kept. I was grateful to be left alone with the chatelaine.

Jessica's red hair had grayed and faded and her face was lined from days and years in the sun, but the bones were classic and the beauty perennial. She brushed back a titian forelock and led me out through the kitchen. "How are you keeping yourself, Matty?"

"Always the same, dear. Nothing has changed for me."

"I guess not." She creased a freckled brow. "Your friend Robin is cute."

"They're all cute."

"Yet I keep hoping for some kind of wedding announcement for your quarter, if only because you're the last of the Sinclairs." I moved closer to her, inhaling stable scents, and remembered when hers was the fragrance of jasmine.

"Perhaps not. I haven't ruled out the possibility of another generation."

"Good. I'm glad there's still hope.

"Chuckie is getting our mounts ready. Most of our horses are trained for English style, but Charles still tries to convert everybody to Western."

"It would be easier to convert me to diesel fuel, dear. Riding on that forty-pound Western saddle is like lying in a cradle in the back of a station wagon. There's just too much between horse and rider."

"So I keep telling him. I'm glad the boys all ride English anyway—mainly because they love to jump fences."

"Without getting gored on that saddle horn."

I followed her through the stable doorway, over which Cowboy had nailed an old horseshoe, tines pointing down so the luck would fall on whoever passed beneath it.

The Eisenhardt stable's thirty box stalls were almost all occupied by extremely sleek and well-kept show animals, some with their latest prize ribbons pinned overhead. Jessica walked down the aisle way to the rear of the stable, stopping a moment to stroke the nose of a black saddlebred. Then, all in one motion, she picked up a hundred-pound sack of sweet feed and hoisted it to her shoulder. I rushed to assist her, but she carried it herself, ignoring my hands.

"It's nothing, Matty. I'm used to this." Letting the sack down, she pulled a penknife out of her jeans and unfolded it. "Why don't you tell me the latest gossip while you're here?"

"What's to tell?"

She used the knife to open the top of the sack, then up-ended it into a steel drum as easily as most women spoon sugar into coffee. "According to Betty's column, you and Edwina Devon have become an item."

"Why would you read Betty's column? You dropped out of the circle twenty years ago."

Yes, it had been twenty years.

They met at the Eye Bank telethon in the spring of '66. Jessica was one of the pretty little academy girls on the phone bank, taking pledges on-camera. Eisenhardt appeared as the most colorful and eloquent of "guest stars." Together they raised thousands for the Eye Bank as well as the temperature of the studio on that first magic evening.

I recalled the great uproar later that summer when Cowboy took this daughter of one of our first families as his bride. The Clouets no longer had money, but their name still meant something. The debutante's love for the rodeo star was called the mismatch of the season.

"I don't brunch at Brennan's anymore, or sip daiquiris under Teri Case's blow dryer. But still sometimes I catch myself reading the society page. That's as close as

I get to the old life." She laughed a little guiltily. "Or want to. I'm tremendously happy here, you know."

"I'm glad, Jessica."

"Oh, Matty, you can't understand how it is with Charles. He's the gentlest man you could imagine."

I had just glanced out the stable door to observe the gentlest man I could imagine split an oak tree trunk clean in half with one blow of a double-headed ax.

"Umph. I'm sure."

"And we have the children, the horses, the land . . ."

"Plenty of company."

"There's that, too." She smiled. "My husband is a wonderful provider. There's plenty of everything for all of us."

"You look happy, dear. That's all that matters."

She did.

Her oldest son, Chuck, walked through the aisle way leading a spirited bay thoroughbred with jauntily braided mane and tail.

"This is Edwina's jumper, Cricket. She said you wanted to take her out this afternoon."

I had to reach up to check her bit, the mare being an impressive seventeen hands high. "Cricket and I are old friends. We'll get along fine."

"Then you know she's one of our most distinguished boarders. Cricket won first prize in the open jumper class at Pin Oak last year."

"She almost pays for herself. Edwina is a fine judge of horse flesh." I automatically ran my fingers under Cricket's girth, which was tight. The Eisenhardt boys were all expert stablehands.

"But she's a bit on the careless side, if you ask me." Jessica checked Cricket's nose strap and clucked at her. "You know how temperamental this girl is. I wouldn't let anyone but an expert rider on a horse like her, and I'd want to see him prove it first."

"Naturally you would. So?" I pulled the left stirrup under my arm to measure it and let it out a notch.

Then I walked around and made the same adjustment for the right as Cricket shook her mane, restless to get going.

"So yesterday Edwina sent over this friend of hers, Billy Oakes. She wanted him up on Cricket."

"Well, he's a big man and she's a lot of horse. They're well matched for size. And he's supposed to be an expert rider."

Jessica raised one exquisite eyebrow. "Matty, when Chuck led this mare out, Mister Oakes took one look at the outfit and his mouth fell right open. For Pete's sake, the man only rides Western."

"Edwina has been sheltered all her life. No one ever told her about Western style."

"Well, Cricket was never even trained for cross-reining, so Chuck had to go right back and saddle Top Man."

"Top Man is used to carrying Cowboy; I'm sure Bill Oakes presented no problem."

"No, Bill loved him—actually tried to buy him from us. Can you imagine? Charles would as soon sell one of the kids." She brushed an insolent fly off the mare. "We're still working on the steeplechase course. But it's good enough to try out. You going to jump today?"

"I'm in the mood. Cricket knows the whole course, doesn't she?"

"Like the back of her hoof. I'm glad you're getting back into it. I remember when you were the best male rider on the Southwest Circuit. Before the accident . . . Poor Domina."

This was in reference to a ghastly spring morning when we were both sixteen. Jessica had been on the scene when my Hanoverian jumper, Domina, lost her nerve halfway across a four-foot fence and threw us both in the dirt.

"No one would blame you for giving up riding. That fall put you in the hospital for six weeks and left you with a permanent head injury."

"I have no complaint about the epilepsy. It kept me out of Nam."

The worst part was that the magnificent Domina had broken her leg, the fore cannon, and had to be put down. I was knocked cold, so don't remember being shoved into the ambulance and sped off to Hotel Dieu Hospital. But it was left to Jessica to call our vet to perform the coup de grace with a rifle shot between the mare's eyes. The end was painless for the mare. Not for me.

Domina had taken fences that height countless times before, in practice and in competition. But the mare was cranky that morning because she was being wormed, and I was such a dribbling hand-job that I insisted she make the jump anyway. I'll always be tormented by the fact that the accident was entirely my own fault.

Domina had been my thirteenth birthday present, and I loved that Hanoverian second only to my mother.

Now Chuckie led out Jessica's favorite gelding, Doc, wearing a custom-fitted English jumping saddle in embossed leather. Doc is a stunning palomino whose golden coat complements the golden red of Jessica's hair. She grabbed mane and climbed on, then quickly urged him onto the path as I swung aboard Cricket and asked her for a posting trot. Her trot was fast and smooth and it took me not a minute to accommodate to her rhythm. I quickly overtook Jessica; she had to move up to a canter to keep ahead, waving toward the scenic route.

The first thing Cowboy had done on settling his land was to plan the bridle path through the woods and across streams. He kept overhanging tree limbs trimmed so that a rider wouldn't get his head knocked off, but most of the brush was as nature intended.

Jessica turned in her saddle to catch my eye. "You'd better skip that first four-foot wall. Charles just dumped some gravel around there to shore it up."

"Are you going to skip it?"

"Not me."

"Then fat chance that I will."

"Are you still looking to beat me, Matty?"

We used to compete in the Combined Training Division. Jessica always outpointed me on dressage, while I beat her in stadium jumping. In cross-country we were about even.

I saw a delicious four-foot stone wall directly ahead. It was still under construction, with bricks and gravel heaped to one side."

"Is that your hazard?"

"Doc takes it without breathing hard. Watch this."

Her palomino headed straight for the center of the wall, tail held high, as though he wanted nothing so much in his life as to jump it. He cleared the obstacle with a good foot to spare. Fortunately. Because a spill would have put horse and rider in a very hard place.

I nudged Cricket's flanks and suggested we follow them at a posting trot. Two strides away from the wall, I took my two-point. But when I clucked a signal to make the jump, she refused and cut to the left. I reined her around in a circle and approached the wall again, this time using a strong right rein and left leg so she wouldn't try the same trick. But now the mare just stopped dead. It was time to wield an angry crop, but I hadn't brought one. Cricket had never balked at a fence before.

Had I lost my touch? I was mortified.

Jessica turned in her saddle and shouted.

"Thought better of that one, Matty? Here's a little three-foot hedge coming up."

There was no mockery whatever but I still felt like a jerk. At least Cricket was willing to do that little bit. Or maybe she was making a small concession, because when I took my jump seat and clucked, she sailed over the hedge as easily as a gazelle. But I didn't.

As my mount reared up to take the jump, her chest expanded and the saddle slid off sideways. And so, unhappily, did I. A split second later, I was rolling in the green grass, wondering what had happened.

In all my years of riding I've had countless falls, and probably spent more time in midair between saddle and ground than most people have astride. But somehow I still haven't mastered the art of landing gracefully. This one jarred every bone from the coccyx all the way up through the spine for a solid whiplash effect.

Jessica heard or felt my cry of outrage and doubled back to meet me. Doc was angry at the interruption to his play.

"What happened, Matty?"

"I fell off a horse. . . . No, I didn't. It was the saddle. But I'm okay. See to Cricket."

"I'll get her." Jessica reined around and took off at a gallop. I had time to stand up brush turf and grass off my jodhpurs before she returned, leading the snorting and disgusted mare.

"I'm so sorry, Matty. The girth seems to have broken. I'm going to punish Chuck for not checking it today."

"I should have checked it myself. Please don't blame your son. There's no harm done."

"You're sure you're all right?"

"Absolutely." I took Cricket's rein. "Go ahead and finish the course. I'll just lead this girl back to the house. I could use the walk."

I didn't expect her to believe me, because nobody could use a walk in riding boots. But I wanted to be alone with the horse.

After a polite protest, Jessica reined Doc back around and jumped the same hedge that had precipitously ended my own ride.

After she had cantered out of sight, I brought Cricket to a halt and checked her girth myself. It had been cut nearly all the way through, right up under the saddle so I hadn't seen it before. Chuck wouldn't have either unless he'd been looking for trouble. And there was no reason he should have been.

If Cricket had been more cooperative at the first obstacle, I would be limping back to the house at best. Maybe I'd still be lying among the bricks and gravel.

Eisenhardt was still occupied with his fencing operation, but on catching sight of my sad little parade, he put down his ax. "What happened to you, Matt?" His lower lip was front-loaded with snuff.

"Equestrious interruptus."

"She th'ow a shoe on you?" He took hold of the bridle. "No, I see it's the saddle. What the hell happened?"

"Nothing much, Cowboy." There was no use telling him of the sabotage. He'd find out soon enough. "I guess the girth just frayed apart. Must be a pretty old outfit. These things happen."

"Too bad. That there was Edwina's favorite close contact saddle."

"It worked. I made close contact with the ground."

He clucked at Cricket and led her back into the stable. "It's a shame, but I got plenty more jumping saddles in the tack room. Let me fix you up."

"No, I've had enough riding for today. How about introducing me to some of these fine animals?"

"Be my pleasure. Chuck!" The diligent home-grown stablehand appeared and took charge of Cricket without comment. My grass-stained condition bore witness to my misadventure and he was too polite to embarrass me about it. Cricket nickered as she was led away and flicked her braided tail, inviting me back for a rematch sometime.

Cowboy picked an apple out of a full bag, then stopped at the first stall and nodded at the inmate.

"This mare here is a hard keeper. Give her five pounds of cracked corn, oats, and whey meal a day and she'll only shake it off. Nervous." He picked up an empty Bio Groom Hoof Polish jar to serve as a cuspidor. "Got to feed her extra beet pulp just to keep her figure. She's worth it, though. The best barrel racer I got."

I followed him through the aisle way, getting a capsule history of the life and achievements of every tenant till we came to the last and largest of the box stalls. The etched and painted sign on the dutch door proclaimed its sorrell resident to be one "Top Man." This gelding needed no title to command respect. He was a bulldog-style quarterhorse at least fifteen hands high and weighing all of 1300 pounds. His back looked broad enough for a man to curl up and take a nap on.

Cowboy quartered the apple and held a piece out in his fist. The horse felt fruit and fingers with his sensitive lips then gingerly wrested the former from the latter and chomped contentedly. "Ol' Top Man won me a lot of prize money back on the circuit for cuttin' and ropin'."

Missy came in to join us, stepping through clumps of hay, and rubbed up against Cowboy like a kitten needing to be stroked.

"Robin is heating up my curling iron. We're going to make me look like Lady Godiva."

"Just so's you don't try to dress like her." Cowboy placed his left hand under her long hair and caressed the back of her neck while continuing with his narrative. She stretched in the crook of his arm and purred.

"You know this horse never drug a calf more 'n a foot and a half in his career. Also, he was my best stud. This here boy bred and settled eighty-five mares in one year."

"Wonder where he got it from."

"Damn shame I had to cut him. But I'm keepin' a lot of mares now, and almost always at least one of 'em's in season. So he got too unruly. Kicked his stall down more'n once. Jumpin' a fence was nothin' to him either. And people bringin' their mares in to board wasn't lookin' for no mongrel foals."

As Missy took leave to keep her date with Robin and

the curling iron, a boisterous greeting sounded from outside.

"Hello there! Hope Top Man is ready for me!"

It was my old friend Geoff Ramsey who yahooed us, swaggering into the stable dressed in full Western gear. The pearl-buttoned gingham shirt and boot-cut Levis fit his physique, if not his personality.

"Howdy, Matt. Edwina told me you'd be riding today."

I shook his hand. "But I didn't know you were."

"Sure. I'm getting a lot of continuances and court has been recessing early almost every day this week. So I can climb into my official Roy Rogers riding outfit and blow on over." He patted his gut. "I developed sort of a fat problem, see. So I'm just letting Top Man jog it off."

I said, "Seems to me, that would only help Top Man's fat problem."

"This weight control measure is predicated on the assumption that a man can't eat a heavy meal while loping along on a quarterhorse."

"Chuck will have him ready for you in a few minutes." Cowboy said. "The old boy could use the exercise as much as you."

"Great." As Geoff brushed at his brand-new Tony Lama boots I wondered if he thought he could assimilate Cowboy's macho and equestrian skills merely by dressing the part, though the effect wasn't quite authentic. He looked rather like third prize winner at a Rotarian Halloween party. "Hey, Matty, Ondine has been asking about you."

"How is Ondine? And the boys?"

"The boys are fine, and Ondine's even better. You know 'Couples Tell' has got a twenty share now?"

"I should know, since I buy time on the show every week. Seems it appeals to a broad segment of the viewing audience."

"That's all Ondine's doing. She gets a good mix of

couples for each taping: one from the sports world, one from show business and one from our crowd."

"Just regular people."

"Right. Look, she told me they're short of talent for this week's taping. Say, Cowboy, you're a famous rodeo rider.'

"Not no more, I ain't."

"You still qualify as a sports figure. Why don't you and your wife go on the show?"

Eisenhardt spit into his cup. "Which wife?"

"Why . . . Jessica, of course."

"Nope. Cain't do it. Geoff. Others'd be jealous."

"I can see your problem." Cowboy stepped outside to get rid of his tobacco, and Geoff turned to me.

"Say, Matty, why don't you and Edwina come to the Plantation House this weekend? The staff is off; the kids are off; and it will only be us sipping tall drinks out on the terrace."

Geoff's Plantation House is an antebellum mansion once built and run by slaves, now fully restored and furnished with period antiques—a counterfeit anachronism with modern plumbing and electrical wiring. The house is set under a bank of oak trees on Bayou La Fourche in the heart of sugar cane country. And I enjoy my occasional weekend there, experiencing the languor and the luxury of a gracious Old South that never was.

"Why not? I could use a little time in the country. And maybe pick up a sack of oysters along the way."

He winked. "I'm counting on it."

"Saturday evening then. But I'll have to ask Edwina."

"No need. I talked to her last night and she's all for it. She said just to clear it with you." He smiled. "She said one room was all you'd need. I think the little gal is serious."

Chuckie led Top Man down the aisle way. I automatically checked the cinch all the way up under the saddle and pulled down the stirrups for Geoff. They were already adjusted for him, which was to be expected as he had probably been the last to use the tack. I held the saddle for him while he hoisted himself aboard.

Then Geoff and Top Man made a silent agreement between them that neither would work too hard and moved along down the bridle path.

Cowboy saw them off with a wave of his hat. "Ridin'll tighten up the man's thighs and butt some, but it can't do nothin' for that belly o' his. That'll just flop."

Carmen brought him his hourly can of Dixie. He used the first swig to wash the tobacco out of his mouth then thanked her with an affectionate pat on her ample rear. That seemed to be thanks enough. She smiled and returned to her kitchen duties.

I supposed that when a man can have three wives he likes some variety among them. So he takes himself a slender blonde, a curvaceous brunette, and a redhead who is just . . . perfect."

"You want somethin' to wet your whistle, Matt?"

"My whistle is fine, thank you."

"Then how's about a tour of the place? You want to see the old grizzly?" On the way out through the stable yard, he picked up a dark-haired toddler (Carmen's), hefted him up on his shoulders, and carried him along for the ride. "Take that trail to your left there. We're going up through the woods."

After about ten minutes of hiking, I said, "This must be a good walk from the house."

"Got to be. I need that bear well upwind when my ladies get their time o' the month. That stuff drives 'im crazy, you know."

"I've read about female hikers getting torn to pieces for walking into the woods on the wrong day."

"Mine know better, though. And anyhow a grizzly is contrary enough when it's in the best o' moods."

A half mile from the stables was a space cleared for the bear's accommodations. Cowboy walked us around a double cage of wrought iron bars attached to a low concrete structure. But there was no tenant in sight.

"Did he step out for a beer?"

"Don't reckon. Brother Bear just went inside to git out of the sun. I don't need a roof on this cage because the walls are twelve foot, and this particular full-growed grizzly can't climb too good."

"You need two cages for the mating?"

"Yep. I'll have to keep the boar in isolation awhile till he gits good an' lonely. Then I move a real purty little sow bear into the cage next door."

"How will you know if she's pretty?"

"Let's face it, she don't have to be *too* fancy to appeal to this good ol' boy. Trouble here is bears like to congregate in mating season—sort of like goin' to a barn dance. Then they can choose their sweethearts. But I can only give this boar one sow to choose from. So I let them git to know each other through the bars." He pulled on one of the bars. "Tempered steel, three inches thick. Even that half-ton grizzly couldn't come through this thing."

"Sounds like teasing."

"Got to make sure his intentions 're honorable, ya know. Sometimes they're unsociable and liable to injure the sow. But once the bear shows he's a gentleman, then I'll open that little door between the cages and let them court. Matin' season is late spring, so the time is good."

"Just uncork the white wine, put on a Johnny Mathis album, and let nature take its course."

"I only got to give them enough privacy. Then if the chemistry is good, we should have ourselves little twin cubs long about January."

"You seem the authority on breeding bears."

"Got my own personal techniques. Bet I can handle any animal goin'—includin' the human female."

"That species especially well."

I had once seen him use his "personal techniques" on Carmen during a particularly loud and fierce altercation. Having learned my own scarce Spanish from Mexican riggers on the Bay of Campeche, I had difficulty understanding Carmen's, which was peppered with Olmec Indian vituperatives, but she seemed to be raging at her husband for the crime of not paying enough attention to her. Her side of the debate was shouted and shrieked and described with manic gesticulation. Cowboy, for his part, simply stood with arms folded smiling down at her . . . until Carmen drew her arm back to slap him. With lightning movement, he caught it in midair.

"*Esperate!*" ("Wait!")

Then he took off his glasses and leaned over her, still smiling.

"*Hagalo pues.*" ("Now go ahead.")

She leaped to the challenge, delivering a blow so forceful that it would have spun my head around three or four times. Cowboy only rubbed his reddening cheek and said, "*Te sientes mejor?*" ("Feel better?")

Apparently she had vented all of her anger with the one slap, because she didn't protest when he scooped her up in his arms and soundly kissed her pouting lips.

"Say, Matt. Me and the old lady got some personal business to take care of. Be back in a bit."

I'd spent the next forty minutes perusing some Frederic Remington drawings of the Wild West while Cowboy finished his "personal business." Then he sent Carmen off to cook dinner, which, as I remember, turned out to be excellent.

Either the sound of our voices or Cowboy's cigarette smoke had awakened the sleeping grizzly, and the brownish buff omnivore stirred and lumbered out of his artificial den to complain. Reared up on his hind legs, the monster was well over seven feet tall, with humped shoulders and claws appearing even longer than his teeth. When he looked at me and sniffed, I backed away from the cage.

"See that hump on his back?" My guide pointed. "Pure muscle it is, powering those front legs. Jaws are strong enough to crush a bull's skull like an egg shell."

"That would be an expensive meal."

"He'll eat anything," Cowboy said. "Insects, roots, fish, rodents, deer, pigs"—he clenched his teeth around his cigarette and laughed—"even fruits. Nothin' personal."

"Thanks."

"Hey now, bears ain't the only critters git fed around here. Y'all will have dinner with us sure. The ladies'll be cookin' up somethin' special tonight."

"I wish with all my heart that I could, Cowboy, but we've agreed to have a long, dull dinner with Reverend Jack Dundy."

"Whaddaya have to say to that TV preacher?"

"Nothing at all. He wants to say it to me, and I promised to listen at seven-thirty."

I hated to leave them early—the horses and Jessica—but it was sheer consolation being driven across Lake Pontchartrain Bridge at dusk, counting off the mile posts under the red sun.

Chapter 7
Wednesday Evening, March 8th

The pretty blond hostess looked like a sixteen-year-old playing dress-up in her white ruffled blouse and ankle-length black skirt. But she swayed with a precocious model's glide through Arnaud's elegant Richelieu Room, showing us to my usual table by the far wall against the cypress wainscotting. When Robin and I took our chairs under the oil painting of La Formidable Lady Irma, the candy box creature smiled and handed us menus, displaying an impeccable manicure. Then she turned gracefully and swished her skirt on the retreat.

I watched her all the way back to her desk in the foyer before studying the bill of fare.

"Here, Robin, why don't you try their Crawfish Wellington?"

"Doesn't this place have any catfish? . . . That preacher likes to keep people waiting." Robin diddled with the vase of fresh red carnations and looked toward the giant front windows, though he couldn't see through the textured glass. "Why did you tell him to meet us here at Arnaud's?"

"The restaurant was his choice."

"You should have told him to come to the Vieux Carre instead. It's only across the street."

"Why the Vieux Carre?"

"Because remember what that delivery man said? If we can be there at *precisely* eight-twenty-three, we'll get to see 'stern master' meet 'naked body slave.' "

"That's the last thing I want to see. You'll get a snootful of depravity later on at the Orangeman."

"Oh, I can't wait. That's going to be my first big-time all-gay orgy."

"It's not supposed to be an orgy."

"Bet I can make it one. . . . What does 'Pompano En Croute' mean?"

"It doesn't mean catfish. You won't find your Goujon Caille in the city, anyway."

"I like the way you cook it in tomato sauce."

"That's Coubillion. But even in my magic hands, it will never be as good as when I was a boy. We used to catch those spotted catfish, clean them, and cook them over a fire right there on the bayou."

"Is this going to be a 'longing for the past' story? I never bore you with that kind of stuff."

"You don't have a past."

"I was a kid, too."

"Growing up on Wonder Bread and 'The Brady Bunch' in southern California doesn't count."

Maybe it's a sign of encroaching middle age when one's childhood memories grow brighter instead of dimmer. I was recalling my lazy summer vacations in Grand Prairie, a small farming community whose commercial center boasted only a cotton gin and a general store. On the hottest July days we whooping, chattering boys would pile into "Nonc" Aldus's pickup for a trip to Bayou Cocodrie.

Aldus Fontenot wasn't really my uncle, but he was related enough not to mind, or notice, one more child's face around the supper table. And there was always room for another boy in the *garconnière*, the loft under the roof that served as the boys' dormitory.

When I arrived at Nonc's every June with my single suitcase, his land had already been plowed and planted. So there was no more farm work to do till the crop was "made" and ready to harvest at summer's end. During the hot vacation months, Nonc Aldus's main industry was fishing. And he was happy to take a few immature but enthusiastic helpers along to carry the pirogue and gather wild pecan wood for the fire.

We used to bait our trot lines with live perch caught in a crawfish seine, not setting them till after sundown, when the striped turtles wouldn't steal the bait. We'd paddle our pirogue along the lines checking "bobbers," the corked jugs that dipped and bounced whenever a fish had taken the hook.

No restaurant meal ever tasted as good as Nonc Aldus's smoke-flavored Catfish Coubillion, cooked on an open fire while we sat listening to his stories of *le vieux temps.*

I made Robin wait to order until our party was complete, which wasn't long enough to starve him. The mass market evangelist arrived only ten minutes late, bowling around fern plants and slender Doric columns with arms out to greet us. I rose as a gesture of respect for his age and debilitated condition and shook his hand. His grip was of the typical two-handed minister's variety.

"Puh-leased to see you here, brother!" he boomed as though my scrubbed and smiling face had just graced his front pew. Then he noticed Robin. "And you too, brother."

Reverend Jack Dundy had a stunning silver toupee and a voice that reverberated like a base drum. All the better to call sinners home to Jesus.

He sat spraddle-legged in his chair and tucked the white linen napkin into his shirt. "The Lord meant for us to enjoy the partaking of food to sustain life. Glory be to the name of Lord." And in this spirit the Lord's obedient servant ordered Crabmeat Cocktail, Oysters on the Half Shell, and Stuffed Quail from the tuxedoed waiter. But he waved off the sommelier with both hands.

"I need neither wine nor strong drink, boy. I'm high on *Jesus!*" The chandelier above his head shook its crystal droplets in a tinkling "Amen."

"I need both wine and strong drink," Robin countered, and grabbed the wine list. "I've been learning all about this from my new book about wine."

"Probably *Snoopy's Guide to Wine Tasting*," I averred. "But at least you've learned difference between white and red. Enjoy them while you may."

The federal government is forcing Louisiana to raise the drinking age from eighteen to twenty-one on pain of losing highway matching funds. There has been a lot of squawking from bar owners who profit from the fuzzy-cheeked crowd. They argue that any man old enough to don the uniform of his country is old enough to get fleeced in its clip joints.

For Robin, it makes no difference at all. He acts equally foolish drunk or sober.

"I'll take that white Burgundy, the Pouilly Fuisse eighty-four. It's a foppish little wine but indomitable in its way."

I saw that his choice was $36 a bottle and intervened.

"You'll have the Beaujolais Blanc and be happy. It's a regional little wine but cosmopolitan in its propensity."

As if he would have known one from the other. I could have served him Ripple in a gallon jug. A domestic little wine but international in its pretension.

The waiter was still waiting so I gave my attention to the list of appetizers while pretending to listen to the holy Reverend.

"You and I don't agree on everything, Sinclair," he allowed grandly. "But I took this evening away from my ministry because I think we can join together in our battle against Satan's forces."

"I'll take the Snails en Casserole to start. . . . Satan?"

"In the guise of legalized gambling. Sin and perdition are all around, brother Sinclair. And now the sin-mongers want to bring us all the decadence of Nero's Rome. We've already got Sodom and Gomorrah."

I decided not to take that personally. "And Oysters

Bienville, Pompano Pontchartrain, and the house salad.
Same for Robin."

"What? I haven't decided yet." My gracious ninny
was still combing the menu for something that looked
like catfish.

"At Catfish Heaven, I'll defer to your judgment. . . .
I'll take the cheese and fruit for dessert, and he'll have
the chocolate mousse."

This last selection earned his purred approval. Robin
would smack his lips over chicken droppings if they
were artistically rolled in chocolate sauce and topped
with whipped cream and sprinkles.

When our wine was served, the Reverend leaned
back in his chair with arms righteously folded to indicate that he was having none of it.

"Jesus turned water into wine," I couldn't help saying.

"No suh. No, he did not. Our Lord Jesus Christ
turned water into *grape juice*. And that's the original
scriptures."

"Why ruin good water?" Robin asked rhetorically,
and sipped his Beaujolais. "A phonetic little wine but
with an eclectic spirit."

"God Himself is watching us closely, though. When
He looked down at sinful New Orleans and saw that
servant of Satan, Brad Rutledge, prepare to tempt the
faithful, you know what He did?"

Robin blinked. "Geez! What?"

"He *smote* him!" And the good Reverend smote the
table by way of emphasis, shaking the flatware and
setting up sloshing waves in the water carafe.

"You think Brad's murder was God's doing?" I asked
with a straight face. "There's a suspect I hadn't even
considered."

"The Lord has his instruments. He guided someone's
hand. Don't doubt it. And you can be one of His
instruments, Sinclair, even though you're but a miserable sinner. That's why I've called you here."

"Reverend Dundy, I think—"

"Jack," he corrected jovially. "Just call me Reverend Jack. Everybody does."

"As you like. But while your group and mine have a common goal, I don't see how we can work together to achieve it."

"Why not? Your hifalutin rich people in their fancy duds appeal to one segment of the population, and my good Christians attract another. Between the two groups we can get a lot of voter support and work some real righteous pressure on the legislature." Then he attacked his Quail au Chambertin as though it were a purveyor of everything base and vile.

"I wonder if you would just like to collect some money from my 'hifalutin rich people.'"

"For such a worthy cause, yes such." The stuffing dropped on his napkin.

"And turn it over to your good Christians for disbursal."

"Bother Matt, we've got the numbers. My followers are poor but dedicated to carrying the word of Christ. With your people's money and my people's inspirational energy, together we can lick this threat of vice and ruination." He looked up at the ivy-draped balcony as though expecting a choir of angels to sing a refrain. But there were only other diners enjoying their à la carte meals without a thought to vice or ruination.

"An upwardly mobile little wine but fetching in its bourgeoisie."

"Shut up, Robin. I'm sorry, Reverend Jack, but I don't subscribe to your philosophy. And any help I give you would only strengthen your organization."

"And what's wrong with that?"

"This month you would be working with me against gambling. But next month you'll be fighting just as hard against every freedom I hold dear." He ruminated over his quail. He had forgotten his teleprompter and had no fit answer in his repertoire, so I picked it up again.

"Reverend, I'm afraid you've taken this evening away from your ministry for nothing. The two of us will never agree on mission or means."

The preacher sighed. "All righty then. If I can't appeal to your love of your savior, then let's talk money. You sell me that riverfront land at current assessed value."

"Current assessed value is a lot less than developers would pay, so why should I sell it to you?"

"Because you know I'll keep gambling out of the area. You see Jesus, came to me in a vision and asked me to build Him a tabernacle there on that very spot. Jesus was a fisherman, just like the poor folk around there."

"Well, you can go ahead and buy Jesus a trawler. The worst thing I could do for 'poor folk' would be to sell that land to you or any other religious group."

"How's that?"

"Because then the property would become tax exempt, and there would be less money coming into the state treasury . . . for the poor folk."

Reverend Jack looked wounded. "I got to say I pity you, brother Matthew. Because you haven't seen the light yet. And I'm personally gonna ask Jesus to lead you back to His fold."

"That won't be necessary. I'm a Catholic."

"Well, that there explains a lot. It surely does." The man of God glanced at his Rolex and stood up. "I've certainly enjoyed our little talk, Sinclair. Unfortunately, I can't stay for dessert. I've got to meet someone across the street at the Vieux Carre." He smiled, showing every cap in his head. "At *precisely* eight twenty-three."

Robin spit wine all over his plate.

Chapter 8
Wednesday Night, March 8th

Mickey Drago's friends had hired the Orangeman Bar on Frenchman Street for the party and auction. The Orangeman, the most popular hangout in the gay ghetto of Faubourg Marigny, is centrally located one block from the Quarter.

Before going inside, Robin stopped under the street lamp to apply a touch of mascara. He studied his reflection in the window of the neighboring book store and batted his eyes experimentally.

"I'm so excited. Everyone's been telling me the kind of fun they have at the Orangeman's parties."

"Don't get your hopes up. This is just going to be one more of those inbred affairs where every man in the room has already been down on every other man in the room."

The rough-trade bouncer saw who I was and waved us into the melange, where the atmosphere was already close and pungent with the small of cooked food and moving, pressing bodies under the dim blue lights.

The Skyliners were wailing on the jukebox:

"I don't have anything, since I don't have you."

And three underdressed gay couples who looked like they didn't have anything anyway were shuffling cheek-to-cheek on the platter-sized dance floor.

I put Robin behind me and churned through the swaying crowd. When at last I found us an air pocket, he looked around like a kid at Disneyland.

"Look at all the fascinating people! Everyone we know must be here. Mickey sure has a lot of friends."

The people Robin in his naïveté saw as chic sophisticates in fetching costumes and naughty postures were only the same desperately lonely misfits who have always populated the city's lurid half-world. Most are forced to keep their real lives secret from the straight society they must live and work in. They have long been estranged from their natural families and are left now with only empty apartments to go home to.

"These aren't friends. They're compulsive party animals. Any one of them would go to the opening of a drain."

The guest of honor was slumped at a table in the rear, trying and failing to register joy and enthusiasm for every well-wisher who came to shake his hand.

Mickey was the most generous man I knew, eagerly offering his time and resources to any cause. He was always the first to volunteer for the neighborhood crime watch, to drive elderly voters to the polls, or to visit the sick with brownies from Laura's and the most stimulating new gossip.

But he had come down with AIDS and now needed visiting himself.

Mickey lost his job working for an optician as soon as his illness became evident. His insurance was inadequate, of course, and medical bills quickly consumed his small savings. In time he had to sell his furniture and appliances to make living expenses, until those too were gone. Three weeks before, Mickey had been evicted from his apartment with little more than a bundle of clothes that no longer fit him.

So now at last the community he had always served so selflessly had united to give something back. A former lover was letting him stay rent-free in a spare room, and all the gay restauranteurs in the neighborhood took turns sending him the daily special. It was tacitly understood that he would not enter their premises.

I went in my own turn to pay him my respects.

"Mickey, you look wonderful!" An absurd thing to say to a dying man. He had lost weight since our last encounter only the month before and looked like a pile of sticks. I hugged him, which I never did before he got sick, because I'm not that warm a person. But now he needed it.

Mickey kept his head down. The burgundy blotches of Kaposi's Sarcoma showed on his withered cheeks.

"Thank you for coming, Matt."

"I wouldn't miss it. Happy to see you again."

I moved aside for the next liar. This was certainly Mickey's last party, and he was so pitiably fatigued that I doubted we should have put him through it. We could have held the auction without him—or better, just taken up a collection.

Don Hilton caught my lapel and pulled me closer. "Oh, Matty?" His breath was hot. "Who is this delicious young fawn you've brought to share with us, you sweet man?"

"Don't feel so lucky, Don. Robin is private stock."

"You're a big meanie. He's the yummiest boy here."

Don (known to *Impact* readers as "mature Greek active") was clad from neck to toe in black leather stretched to shapelessness, scuffed and cracking. I am old enough to remember when the costume was new and poor Don still looked good in it.

Don is a defrocked Anglican priest who has made a literary reputation declaring that the Christian God really loves us homos after all. In a typical conversation, he cites chapter and verse from the Good Book to support his contention. Literally.

"Samuel eighteen, verse one," he announces with one finger upraised. " 'The soul of Jonathan was knit to the soul of David, and Jonathan loved him as his own soul,' right?"

"Male pair bonding," I tell him. "You don't think all army buddies are making it in their bunks?"

"Not all. But there is a lot more going on in army barracks than you may think." Inevitably, he tries again. "And God knows Ruth and Naomi were awfully close for in-laws. 'Whither thou goest. . . .' Hah!"

"Ruth was a stranger from a foreign tribe. She had nowhere to go but with Naomi."

"She could have found her way back to the Moabites if she'd wanted to." Then comes the always absurd clincher. "And what about John fourteen, twenty-three? During the last supper, 'One of his disciples whom Jesus loved lay close to the breast of Jesus.' "

"It was an idiomatic phrase." I respond with uncharacteristic patience. "In that time, people ate reclining on couches and put out their right hands to take the food. So the man to your right was 'at your breast.' It didn't mean you were cuddling the fellow."

"You take the same position as the bigoted and misinformed homophobes. But the Bible itself speaks for us."

"Say, Don, what about that little squib that goes, 'He who lies with a man as with a woman shall commit an abomination'?"

No one should argue theology with a man trained by the Jesuits. Only a muddle-headed Protestant would try.

So he tries.

"Those were only proscriptions against homosexual orgies as practiced by pagans. The true love of one man for another was never condemned in the Holy Bible."

Meanwhile, Don expresses his own "true love of one man for another" by strapping selected fat queens to his coffee table and shaving their heads.

(My own religious philosophy is simple. God must love queers or he wouldn't have made so many of us.)

I was spared our usual exchange now because Don was off his soap box this evening, being more interested in a young man at the buffet who wore skin-tight jeans and a T-shirt announcing "I DON'T HAVE AIDS!" (but this was a very old shirt).

He pointed his beer stein. "I think Barry and I are going to share a beautiful experience."

Barry calls himself an Orthodox Jew and insists upon wearing a yarmulkah all the time, even to bed. But he has an unbelievable pectoral development.

"I'm happy for you both."

The revelry was too loud for whispering. Don kept it confidential by shouting close to my ear.

"I'm having a little problem understanding him, though. I know he wants a sincere, loving relationship, as I do, but he keeps hinting around about discipline."

"So what's the problem?"

"Just that I haven't figured whether he wants to whip me or for me to whip him. I'd hate to do the wrong thing and offend him. What do you think?"

"Easy. Just get out your trusty cat o' nine tails and have at him. Either he'll stretch out and enjoy it or he'll snatch the whip away and start using it on you. One way or the other, you'll know."

"Ooh, and that's just what I'll do. Thank you, Matty. You're better than Ann Landers."

"My pleasure."

Clark Fidey hovered around the buffet table furtively dropping slices of roast beef into a small shopping bag. His hands were so busy filching that he had to wave with an elbow.

"Welcome to the party, Matt. There's a fine selection here. Indisputably."

"I hope I have a chance to taste it."

Fidey was a research librarian at the Mint, and I knew him as probably the best real estate historian in the South. He could tell you the period of every building in New Orleans and pinpoint the decade each wing was added and each addition made. But he'd made himself even better known as the biggest mooch on the Delta. The man obtained his clothes through the courtesy of Volunteers of America. And concerning his choice of colors, it is only charitable to note that it's very dark inside those parking lot dumpsters late at night.

Although, so far as I know, Fidey was heterosexual; he attended every gay event he could get into, not just for the catering but to seek a no-cost sexual outlet. Women require that money be spent on them, if only a dollar for coffee and beignets. And this extravagance is unthinkable for a man of Fidey's frugal turn of mind. Unfortunately, having neither looks, youth, nor charm, he found it difficult to mooch a blow job even in this easy crowd.

"How is work on the third floor?" I asked.

He shifted the bulging bag under his arm.

"Always the same. History never changes."

"There's always something new to learn from it, though."

"I remember when you were up there all the time, tracing your genealogy. You were better than any non-professional I know."

"Thank you. But I never got farther back than the eighteenth century."

Fidey went to jam a deviled egg into his mouth, then, patting his large stomach, thought better of it and instead took a swig of the Maalox he kept at the ready in his bag.

"Most people stop at the War Between the States. This being New Orleans, they're afraid of what they'll find."

Sampling one of the eggs, I heard a snatch of typical party dialogue behind me.

"Honey, my hemorrhoids are so bad you can screw me and say the rosary at the same time!"

"But I'm a Methodist."

A waiter put down a tray of stuffed bell peppers and Fidey jumped for it.

I slid through the crowd around Errol Rose, who sat

astride a barstool holding court amid a circle of chickens. One of our city's few internationally known artists, Errol has achieved recognition with his high-resolution photographs celebrating the bizarre and the grotesque in stark light and shadow. Deformities are his special love, and he has depicted every variety in every configuration.

Someone handed him a can of Ethyl Gaz aroma spray, which he inhaled before waving at me.

"Matty? Have you ordered my latest book, *Twisted Images*?"

"Not yet, Errol. To tell you the truth, I'm not really gone on naked black dwarves."

"Check it out. This one features naked *white* dwarves. And with tattoos!"

"I can't wait. Thank you."

I passed Lennie Muntz, who was probably cross-dressing these days, this being evident from his plucked eyebrows and the pimply complexion caused by heavy pancake makeup.

He balanced a buffet tray on his knees while mewing tales of his workaday world to a fellow drag queen.

"So this here stupid trick didn't want chains or handcuffs. Oh NO-ooo. That would be too easy. It had to be ropes all the way. And I had a *bitchy* time with those knots, getting them tied all around his arms, down his chest to his legs. They all had to be just so. What am I? A goddamn Boy Scout?"

His companion nodded over the quiche. "I hate those fantasies that come in exact minute detail."

"Me, too." Lennie dangled a wrist. "And guess what? After I spent a good half hour setting him up, all on straight time, this asshole tells me, 'I have to go to the *bathroom.*' I was livid!"

"So did you untie him!"

"I didn't have to. It was *his* bed."

Pierre the toy vendor called me over to his favorite

place at the bar. (His elbow prints are in the wood.)
"Yoo-hoo, Matty. Isn't this a scrumptuous party?"

"Apart from the sadness of the occasion."

"We hardly get together anymore, what with the
health scares," Pierre said ruefully. "Everyone's afraid
to go out. . . . Say, I saw that silver thing you donated."

"A Dagobert Pèche silver bowl," the salesman in me
said automatically. "An original, not one of my repros."

"I don't know much about that stuff, but it looked
real nice. Hey! You want to see what I'm giving?" He
reached into his sample case and brought forth a braided
whip. "My most popular item here, imported from
Spain. Hand-tied out of oiled garment leather." He
snapped it lustily in thin air. "The handle is carved to
fit a man's grip and balanced with a jeweler's precision.
Care to try it?"

"No thanks."

"You'll never know until you try."

To spare myself an argument, I took his prize and
slapped my thigh with it. "Sorry, Pierre. It hurts rather
more than I would like."

"Yeah, it hurts a lot," he said proudly and seized the
instrument of pain with both hands. "This is for someone who is really far advanced into S and M. But if
you're a beginner, you could just start with a nice
teaser." He held up a padded leather paddle that fit
over his hand like a baseball glove. "I've got some that
only sting a little."

"Actually, anything tougher than a knotted shoelace
is too harsh for me. I prefer my pleasures unmixed."

He laughed loudly, shaking his earcuffs.

Just wait till you get to be my age. You'll need the
extra stimulation—to do the same old things with pretty
much the same old people." He shrugged and momentarily looked like a same old thing himself. Then he
brightened again. "Whoa, look who I'm talking to here.
A chicken hawk like you has got his own kind of thrills."

"I am not a chicken hawk."

Pierre squinted through the thickening fog of cigarette smoke.

"No? How old is Robin?" I didn't tell him because he already knew. "I suppose you love him because you got so much in common, huh?"

"I love him because . . ."

Because I have to love someone and he loves me. But I would never say that aloud.

Anyway, Pierre wasn't waiting for an answer, having already slipped back into his spiel.

"Say, I've got some new tit clamps here to fit every taste. You can have your choice of Japanese, French, or Australian."

"What's the difference?" As if I cared.

"The Japanese are rubber-tipped, just a little tighter than clothespins. You can use them on anyone."

"I doubt it."

"Then the French ones are metal-tipped. They hurt."

"I would imagine so. Yes."

"The Australian tit clamps are the best." He licked his lips. "They have claws."

"Ouch."

A well-built young waiter passed among us wearing a red leather bow tie and matching harness. Nothing else.

"Would you gentlemen like some liquid refreshment?"

"Right here, sweetums." Snapping whips is thirsty work and Pierre appropriated a tall drink. "I've got a special sale on, Matt. Could I interest you in a metal ball press?"

"Nobody could."

Just then Robin appeared on my left, tugging my arm.

"I just played our song. Can't you hear?"

It was coming from the juke now: Luther Vandross's version of "A House Is Not a Home." It was Robin, not I, who had designated this the anthem of our relationship, but tonight the verse seemed most appropriate.

I'm not meant to live alone.
Turn this house into a home.
When I climb the stair and turn the key,
Oh please be there. . . .

I leaned against the bar and gazed around at our friends and neighbors, the "queers" and the outcasts, all expatriates of middle America. Raised in a society that had made no place for them, they compulsively sought a counterfeit acceptance night after night in passionless promiscuity. (What asshole ever decided to call these people "gay"?) And wouldn't I be just as self-destructive as they if I didn't at least have Robin and our parody of a family to come home to?

I put my arm around his shoulder and drew him to me for a kiss on the lips, a normal gesture only in this abnormal place. He snuggled against me gratefully because I'd never before shown him any affection in public.

But even as I was holding him I thought about Edwina Devon, contrasting her with Robin and the sunlit straight world with this dark, inglorious one.

If I ever had the choice, would I change?

Were there any choices?

He rested against my chest. "Let's dance, Matty?"

"Later maybe." A lie.

He understood that and drew away peevishly.

"I don't care. Felix just invited me to go to the can with him."

"You're *my* date, you little slut."

"Not for sex. He's got some coke in there. He wants me to snort a line."

"You do and I'll break your nose."

"Ooh, I *hate* it when you're macho." He wriggled his little round butt and turned away.

"You're dopey enough on a 'natch'!" I called, and watched to be sure he didn't go toward the men's room.

Ralph Weitzel was dressed in an authentic-looking police uniform complete with badge and billy club, but you could tell at a glance that he wasn't really on the force. The man is one of Errol's star models and stands less than four feet tall. Ralph never lacks for close friends, though, because he is a tripod.

"Hey, Matty. Mickey looks pretty bad. Right?"

"Very Bad. Two months maybe."

"You an expert?"

"We'll all be experts before long. Mickey's the fifth man I know to catch it."

"How about you? You worried?"

"Not yet. Robin and I had the ELISA test and we're both clean."

"Or you were when you got here." He chortled, looking like a weird Gahan Wilson cartoon. "What would you do if you caught it?"

"I have a thirty-eight caliber cure in my desk drawer."

"That's what we all think before it happens to us. But maybe you'd want to hope like Mickey. Maybe you'd want to hold on till the last minute."

"For some brilliant French guy to come riding up on a white horse with a magic elixir?"

"That's what everybody at this party hopes for."

The auction was successful. Every man present spent more than he could afford on the lots offered. My Dagobert Pèche silver bowl went for twenty percent over market to some tie clerk who would be lunching on beans and rice the next two months to pay for it.

I overpaid for a 1984 Mardi Gras poster that would go nicely in the men's room at the shop, and Robin blew his allowance on a Malayan tapestry that wouldn't go with anything.

The hors d'oeuvres and the ice had run out, the

dance floor was empty, and poor Mickey was asleep at his table. I took Robin's arm.

"Let's go, kitten. It's time to drift off into the night."

"But we can't leave yet, Matty. Errol said he's going to throw money."

"What are you nattering about? Errol has never thrown so much as a carnival doubloon in his life."

"That's what you think. But he told me he's going to give a golden shower. Right from that barstool there."

"Let's go."

"You don't think he meant it?"

"I *know* he meant it."

When we got outside, the street was still busy with the drunk and the dangerous. Robin was still pink with exhilaration.

"Wasn't that a fabulous party?"

"It was successful in its purpose. Poor Mickey collected enough cash to last him the rest of his life."

Hmmph.

"Everybody just adored your silver bowl."

"Yes. I wonder how I'm going to top it for the next auction. And then the one after that."

On arriving home I took the hibachi out to our courtyard to roast the next day's coffee, as is my habit, because I don't want to fill the kitchen with smoke. Also, I like to have this time alone.

Measuring *à l'oeil,* I poured a quarter pound of Ethiopian Mocha Harar beans into my cast-iron skillet. Conventional recipes purport that this amount will furnish "twenty cups of rich, delicious coffee." Twenty for a Yankee maybe. I get eight or ten.

As commercial roasters do nothing but give the beans a tan, I use my special coffee-roasting skillet, which has never been washed and has built up a fine layer of oils and resins. I cook the beans slowly to a French roast, dark brown going on black.

I shuffled and stirred the beans with a long metal spoon. The cold wind blew the thick smoke toward the

Mississippi, five blocks to the west. I moved out of the smoke's way and let the wind whip my shirttails around me.

And I enjoyed the blessed solitude and the freedom to think about life. Not in general. Just mine.

What vital stats would go into my dossier? Matthew Arthur Sinclair, male Caucasian, thirty-eight years old, five feet nine and a half, one hundred and fifty-five pounds. Dark hair going gray but still stuck in tight. Good Catholic education. Financially secure. (Every year it gets easier to make money and harder to make love.)

No wife. No children. That means no grandchildren either. Ever. After I'm gone, it will be as though I never existed.

I hate those words *ever* and *never*.

I took the skillet off the fire. The beans were roasted as far as they could go without burning. I would grind them in the morning just before brewing.

Robin opened the screen door and called out.

"Matty! Edwina Devon is on the phone. You want to take it?"

"Yes. I do."

Chapter 9
Thursday Afternoon, March 9th

After a no-martini, no-fun business lunch, I was met at the door of the shop by Steve, who waved a pink phone memo.

"Lucille Dooley called. She said you know her."

"Not in the biblical sense. Lucille runs the Blue Garden on Decatur Street."

"I know.—I mean, so I've been told. She said she wanted to redecorate her entire establishment. I figured there was a big profit potential there, so I told her you'd drop by."

"Why didn't *you* drop by? She may have some free samples lying around."

"I *offered* to drop by in that very hope, but she requested that you drop by yourself. Said she trusts your sense of style."

"Then I'll drop by."

The Blue Garden is not a garden at all, but the most notorious establishment on the city's most infamous street. The "hostesses" who work therein can spot a full wallet through a seaman's trouser pocket a block away at midnight in a rainstorm. Within scant seconds, they're up and out of the bar, rubbing their sticky hands all over the mark, asking if he'd like a "party." The type of "party" offered doesn't involve hors d'oeuvres and funny hats, but is usually simplified to a watered drink at the front bar and a quick trip upstairs.

Upstairs, our earnest seaman will find a claustrophobic room with an old collapsing bed and a young collapsible girl. There he will experience a quick wash in a leaky sink followed by a bounce on the old springs.

How do I know all this?

Don't ask.

The proprietress, Lucille, is a brassy pop-eyed woman I hardly know and like less. But this afternoon she greeted me effusively, mixed my Sazerac with real Wild Turkey, and served it in a clean glass.

I tasted her effort. "You went heavy on the bitters."

She leaned over the chipped Formica bar. "So don't complain. It's free, ain't it?" Her neckline drooped so low that I could have seen her dugs if I'd wanted to. I didn't. "We're gonna add a little class to this place, ya know? Then maybe we can attract a tonier clientele. The uptown crowd."

I sipped at the concoction even though it was excessively strong. "Much as I would like to make a sale, I must advise against it."

"Against what? Huh?"

"Lucille, an investment such as you propose would be ill-advised. Uptown johns use call services. They wouldn't come slumming in this section of the Quarter just for the furniture. Not if Brooke Shields were lying around on it."

She shrugged as though it wasn't her money anyway. And it probably wasn't.

"I want one of them fancy brass beds with the curtains, see?"

"Brass beds don't come with curtains."

"Then we'll start a new fad. Come look at one of the rooms upstairs."

"I can tell you exactly what's up there without looking. You have a three-drawer dresser with seven layers of paint, a splintering night stand, and a bed that no sober person could sleep in."

"Yeah, that's right. So we move the old furniture out, get in some wallpaper, some rugs. Give the girls a nice place to work, you might keep 'em longer. C'mon."

Lucille took my stiff, reluctant hand in her clammy one and yanked me up the steep and narrow steps to the second floor. I carried my drink at arm's length, fearful that the dry cleaning bill for my cashmere blazer would wipe out any possible profit.

She pushed open the first door without knocking, fortunately, not interrupting a game of passion this early in the evening.

"What do you think some fancy wallpaper would do for this, huh? I seen some that's red with girls in G-strings all over it."

I finished the drink, even though it wasn't very good. I needed it. "Lucille, you should consult another type of dealer."

"What type you mean?" She quickly took the glass from my hand, as though fearing I would steal it or break it.

"One whose taste harmonizes with your own. You know that commercial on TV where the announcer dresses like an upholstered chair?"

"Yeah, but—" I didn't hear anything after the "but" because suddenly my head was pounding. The room whirled around me and I fell, crashing full-length across the grimy floor.

I was left with only breath enough to mumble, "You drugged me!"

The woman came to stand over me, the pointed toe of her shoe playing through my hair.

"Uh huh. Used my best bourbon, though. Yes I did."

When I regained consciousness, I saw that I had been moved from the public "private" room. Through dry and bleary eyes, I perceived an armoire overflowing with cocktail dresses and a litter of female toiletries. This had to be Lucille's own living quarters. From the angle at which I viewed the Greater New Orleans Bridge in the fading light of dusk, I guessed we were on the third floor.

"Watch out. He's comin' to."

"S'okay, Wolin. I fixed him tight so he ain't goin' nowhere. And they won't leave marks, neither."

My arms were stretched out and tied to the brass bed rails with cheap polyester neckties in colors I wouldn't wear under any other circumstances.

Lucille was nowhere to be seen. In her place were three individuals who looked even worse: oily, pasta-fed, and reeking of garlic.

The greasiest of the three leaned over me and brushed my lapel, which needed no brushing.

"How you feelin'?"

I had seen him before. "Not my best."

"He can talk now," the one by the door said.

"Yeah, Wolin. You go stand in the hall. We don't want no horny sailors stumblin' in on our business."

"Be right outside, Gino." The door opened and closed, and then there were two. And now I remembered the dark vulture-like features and my "appointment in Samarra".

"It was you who followed me from the Royal Sonesta, Monday."

"Yeah, we were gonna get you in the car and this all woulda been over with real quick. But then you hadda spook and run away from us . . ."

"Runs like a cat on fire," his companion offered.

". . . Necessarily postponin' our interview."

"Sorry for the inconvenience," I said without an ounce of sincerity.

Gino shrugged. "So we hadda do this more subtle-like. Enlisted Miss Dooley's gracious cooperation an' here we are."

"Together at last."

He patted my shoulder. "You wonderin' why we axed you to join us?"

"I'm not a nosey person."

"We can all appreciate that, Mister Sinclair. But we got to confer wit' you. See, we got a little real estate deal goin'. And we need a certain piece of the riverfront."

"Sorry, but I can't get involved."

Greasy smiled with half his mouth. "We know that there lot in question is Sinclair property, and so we're gonna buy it from you, a nice way or a nasty way."

"The land you speak of is my mother's."

"Yeah, but you got legal disposal of it whilst she's in Europe. We got all the facts. So you're gonna sell the lot to us for a nice fair price, even if maybe you don't think it's so fair right now."

"I detect a nuance of threat."

"Yeah, me and my colleagues here got us a whole shitload a nuances."

"Then listen to some free legal advice. Any signature obtained under duress can't be upheld in a court of law."

"Ain't no duress here. 'Ey, Fanetti? You see any duress?" His companion shook his head to agree that there wasn't. "My colleague back there is a qualified notary republic." Fanetti held up a notary seal to show how qualified he was. "And plus, countin' Wolin and Lucille, we got three witnesses here so it'll be real legal."

Greasy grinned then at the tidiness of it all. What he hadn't said was that there would be no contesting the deed transfer on grounds of duress. Because I wasn't to leave the premises alive.

"I won't sign."

"You won't be a little reasonable? That's dumb. But you lose anyhow, Sinclair. 'Cause your dear sweet mama is bound to come home for the funeral, and I think she'll be a lot easier to talk to than you."

And I thought, Let mother handle you. She's a lot tougher than I am. But what I said was, "Blow me away and everyone is going to come looking for you boys."

"Hey no, man. Not us. You're going to blow yourself away."

Fanetti put down his notary seal and produced his

second prop, a glassine envelope bulging with white powder.

"Just what you ordered, Gino—eighty-three percent pure." He tossed the bag to Gino, who held it over my face.

"Now here's how the authorities are gonna see it. Matt Sinclair, this up and comin' young rich guy, is a high liver, see? Runs in the fast lane. He drinks. He dances. He sucks cocks."

"Right," I said. "So what?"

"So also sometimes he snorts a few lines of coke for recreational purposes only."

"Never in my life."

" 'Ey, you kept it a secret." Gino smiled guilelessly, holding his palms out. "Your friends and loved ones will be shocked when you're found OD'd out on the levee. But nobody's gonna kick about it. You're just the type . . . Gimme a mirror."

Fanetti passed him a smudgy hand mirror from Lucille's cluttered dresser and Gino placed it on his lap, under the paunch. Then he snapped the envelope smartly with his thumb and forefinger and emptied it onto the mirror.

"This here is twenty milligrams, almost pure coke. You think that'll be enough, Mr. Sinclair?"

"*I'll* say it will."

"We can't inject it because that would leave a mark. So we do it the stylish way." Gino reached behind him and Fanetti slapped a crisp $50 bill in his hand, which he then rolled into a tight cylinder. "Yer lucky, know it? If I ever get taken out, I hope this here's the way they do it. Hear me, Fanetti?"

Fanetti laughed, wheezing. "Nah. You ain't worth it."

Gino laughed too. "Listen, Sinclair, how about you just take one big snort and enjoy the hell out of it."

'All right." I mimed insouciance. "Here's to one last good time. What have I got to lose?"

"Now yer talkin'."

I discreetly filled my lungs with air, preparatory to spraying the vile stuff all over him and the walls. But just as he was lifting the mirror into huffing and puffing range, Fanetti divined my intention.

"Lookit! he's gonna blow the shit all over you!"

"Goddamn, yer right. We got a smartass here." Gino put down the mirror and drew back his fist.

"Don't," Fanetti warned. "Don't hit him in the face."

"No, don't," I concurred. "I *hate* that."

"What the hell do *I* care if he hates it or not?"

"It'll leave a mark, asshole."

"Never mind then. Just give me the tape."

The ever prepared Fanetti tossed him a reel of three-inch-wide adhesive tape.

"Didn't want to fuck with this," Gino explained, tearing off a four-inch strip. " 'Cause now I got to scrub the sticky stuff off you with alcohol while you're still alive or there might be a red mark."

He used both hands to place the tape across my mouth and rubbed it all around to make a seal. "But now there's only one way to breathe and that's through your nose. So you oughta just lie back and enjoy this pure quality coke."

He rolled up the bill again and tapped it against the mirror. "I almost envy you, Sinclair. Here's a little taste of heaven on your way to the real thing." He unwrapped a single-edged razor blade and arranged the pile of powder into neat little lines, as though preparing refreshments for a party. But I was the party.

Gino aimed one end of his $50 tube at the first line and the other at my left nostril, solicitously, like a mother about to feed a sick child. But nothing happened.

Fanetti told him why. "He's holdin' his breath."

"Can't do it forever."

But I tried my level best and must already have turned a good bright red by the time I heard the door creak open.

"Careful now, Gino," came a voice I didn't expect to

hear. It was the outside man, Wolin, sounding cool as a glacier. "Just put that mirror down on the floor and turn around."

The command was obeyed with palpable hesitation. And then there was a moment of frozen silence. When I dared at last to breathe again, I saw that Wolin's interference was motivated at least in part by the barrel of the automatic held a steady two inches from his left temple. On the other end of it was delicious little Lawrence Dale, who, by the deadliness of his tone, seemed to have aged ten years.

"Pull that tape off him."

Wolin didn't dare move his head, but his eyes darted crazily.

"Listen, DiMarco. You don't have any interest in this."

DiMarco. I remembered that was Dale's original name.

"I have plenty. The tape." The tape was ripped off quickly, leaving a sting. "Did you snort any, Matty?"

"No. I'm all right."

"Gino, this man has nothing to do with our kind of business. Turn him loose. Now!"

Gino was too scared to fumble with the knots and used his razor blade to cut the ties off my wrists. I had to rub the circulation back, but Gino was right. They hadn't left any marks.

"There, see? Your man isn't hurt."

"That's good, *compagno*—good for your state of health and well-being. You itching to start a war? Our army is a whole lot bigger than yours."

"Look, I know that. We don't want no trouble with the Sacci family."

Dale pointed the gun at his groin. "Then you be Sinclair's life insurance policy. If he so much as gets a nosebleed, then I won't like it, and my people won't like it."

Gino and Fanetti exchanged a guarded look then shrugged.

"Whatever you say, DiMarco. We won't touch him."

"Now, crawl back under your rock and leave us alone."

The unholy trio didn't stay to protest that, after all, we were in their place, but filed out the door meekly as ducks in a row. After hearing them rumble down the two flights of stairs, I dizzily rolled off the bed and staggered across the room to watch them from the window. I saw the tops of their heads walk out on the banquette below, saw them make excuses to one another and then move down Decatur Street toward Canal.

Dale-DiMarco locked the door and put the safety on his automatic. "I guarantee they won't be bothering you again. My pop is bigger than their pop."

But I didn't take in a full lung's worth of air until all three were out of sight. Only then did I pull down the stained and wobbly shade and turn back to my rescuer.

"Thank you, Lawrence, though I never thought I'd have reason to thank you for anything."

"You're very welcome." He took off his Perry Ellis trench coat and laid it on the bureau. "I was just keeping a brotherly eye on you, brother. When you blundered into this dive, I gave it an hour then checked to see what was happening." He slipped out of his suit jacket and unknotted his tie. "Lucille's full of news when she's got a gun to her tit."

"Give me a professional opinion. Do you think their faction might have killed Brad Rutledge?"

"I don't." He moved over to the bed and sat on it, bouncing to test the springs.

"Is that your candid view or only the famous 'code of silence'?"

"It's not *omertá*, just common sense. Gino's group wanted exactly what Rutledge wanted. So why bother him? They would have let him go to all the expense of building his casino and then muscled in later. That's their method of operation." He turned down the bedspread. The sheets, at least, were clean. "Let's not waste the room, shall we?"

"What's that supposed to mean?"

He seemed to grow younger again and softer by the second. His big green eyes reproached me.

"Wouldn't you say we're even, Matty?"

"Even? You tried your darnedest to kill me twice. Now you've saved me once."

"We're half even then." He unbuttoned his shirt and let it slide to the floor: "And half. What do you say?"

His body was still youthful but well muscled, with a gymnast's definition.

And I should be ashamed of what I did next.

But I did it so well.

Chapter 10
Thursday Evening, March 9th

Having not walked but run home from Lucille's Blue Garden, I dove immediately into my old-style claw-footed bathtub. I was there ensconced, washing away the cares and sins of the day, when Robin came into the bathroom without knocking, carrying the cordless receiver.

"You've got a call from Sam, your pharmacist."

I wiped my hands on a monogrammed velour towel and took the phone.

"Hi, Sam."

"Matty, I just analyzed those pills Robin brought over, and now I know what your problem is."

"I need more phenobarbital?"

"No, you just need *some*. These aren't the pills I dispensed for you. What you've been taking are chalk and saccharine imitations. Same size and color."

"Is there any way one of your employees could have—?"

"None!" He sounded testy. "I fill all your prescriptions myself."

"Sorry. You know I trust you absolutely."

"Forgiven. Listen, I think someone at your end is pulling a switcheroo. Look around you."

"I guess I know where to look, too." I bid him good-bye and handed the receiver back to Robin. "Remember the cigarette smoke?"

"Yeah, but Sigrid promised not to smoke in the house again."

I hauled myself out of the tub and splashed over to the medicine chest.

"She never had. She was covering up for her boyfriend."

"Lewis Wofford?"

"The way I figure it, Sigrid must have been letting that bum in the house to conduct their primitive mating rites while we were away."

"You sure?"

"That's why Blanche scratched up the back door. Sigrid had to lock her out in the courtyard."

"She would have eaten Wofford alive."

"Because she's an excellent judge of character. Like any head, our uninvited guest couldn't resist checking the household drug supply." I took out my prescription bottles and juggled them from hand to hand.

"He stole your phenobarbital?"

'And substituted counterfeits so I wouldn't suspect. Until I started having seizures."

"What should I do about Sigrid?"

I was gratified at his use of the first person singular. The boy was actually taking on a responsibility.

"Give her two weeks severance and get rid of her. Then change the locks."

"What if she asks for a reference?"

"Don't make me laugh." I tossed him the bottles. "Drive down to Sam's and get me some real pills. I'm going to walk to the club."

The Pyrrhus Club is archaic, an old-fashioned athletic and social retreat where rich white Christians go to meet their own kind and get away from the other kinds, perhaps to get away from real life itself. I am not an elitist, but family tradition dictates that I pay my $2000 dues each year. The Pyrrhus Club was founded by a few rich Creoles in the early nineteenth century, and there has always been at least one Sinclair among the membership.

I try to make it three evenings a week to work out on the Nautilus machines and then swim some laps or play a little handball if I can find a partner. And sometimes in my never-ending quest for aerobic fitness, I become absolutely desperate for a good match.

The depths to which I'll sink for a decent game was evident that night—I had resorted to playing a Yale man named Robert Barber III. Bob's family fortune is one generation old and was made by his father, a trucking contractor named Roberto Barbera. The older man has calluses on his hands and a fourth grade education. And the worth of three like his son. But Barbera wouldn't be admitted to membership in this club. Not that he would ever care to join.

Like most new arrivals, Barber's ambition is to close the door right behind himself, as he indicated while pounding the ball against the wall of the handball court with much more force than necessary.

"Say, Matt. They told me you were voting to let George Fieldstone in."

I caught a seventy-mile-an-hour rebound and slammed it back.

"Absolutely. He's brilliant, civic minded, and has wonderful manners. George'll be an asset to the club."

"But the man . . ." He looked away as if putting all his concentration on the game. Nobody likes to admit he's a bigot unless he's safe in the company of other bigots. "His name wasn't always Fieldstone, you know."

"Some of the nicest people anglicize their names. It's a sign of insecurity maybe, but not of bad character"

He turned redder than his exertions warranted, and well he might. "Listen, it's what he is, Matt. His background, his heritage, are very different from ours." Barber pounded the ball so hard that he had to duck it himself. "I've got nothing against Fieldstone personally, understand; he's a fine man. But if you let him in, you'll have to let the others in, too—the pushy, loudmouthed ones in cheap suits."

New Orleans society was a very tight circle until recently. The old families used to take bloodless delight in keeping all ethnics out of the prestigious Carnival krewes like Rex and Comus. Much is made of the "kings" of the myriad Mardi Gras parades, who are elected by krewes, societies often made up of empty-headed bluebloods and social hustlers. And much is made of them.

Boasting no more than this thin plebiscite, the "kings" come to "think themselves" as the Cajuns say—think themselves royalty for real. The chosen ones are dressed up in royal costumes with wig, makeup, and scepter. And outfitted thus, they climb onto a truck float and ride through the streets seated upon an elaborate throne, waving majestically. The Carnival crowds, caught up in the grandiosity of the occasion, fall all over themselves for the tin doubloons and plastic beads thrown from the floats. The crowds represent the starving peasants of yore who come to pay homage to and seek favors from the anointed.

Inflexible membership requirements excluded even the most eminent of Jews and other disfavored ethnics from taking roles in the pageantry. Until recently they dealt with the issue by leaving town during Mardi Gras week. But a few years ago some of the disenfranchised determined to start a new krewe of their own with nothing but money and enthusiasm. The innovators decided that they would make a big impression fast by paying vast quantities of bucks to national celebrities to serve as feature attractions. And in 1968, on the Saturday before Mardi Gras, the Krewe of Bacchus rolled on its maiden voyage.

The arrivistes were smart enough and rich enough to elect the "King of Jesters" himself to ride their float of honor. And there was much whispering behind fans about the fact that their first parade king was a Jew.

His Majesty Danny Kaye's ride down Canal Street drew the largest crowd ever, and he was the jolliest, most entertaining Carnival king who ever reigned. To date. Though Bacchus's celebrities still make theirs the most popular parade every year.

"Where do you draw the line?" Bob wanted to know.

I had to say it. "They used to draw the line at Italians."

That worked. Barber, né Barbera, missed the next ball, which bounced into the corner and died. "My mother's Irish."

"Irish is worse. Anyway, I don't want to tear the walls down. All I ask is that we judge our prospective members on an individual basis."

"You propose a so-called 'meritocracy.' You would let anyone in without regard to race, color, or creed?"

"It will make a better club, more interesting anyhow. I've been going snowblind around here."

"I just have a reverence for our religious traditions, that's all."

"As an Italian, you should be aware"—I retrieved the ball— "that it was the Romans who did it."

"Did what?"

"Killed Christ."

With that, I slammed the ball so hard that it went past him and bounced off the back wall. He didn't try to return it but let it dribble itself to a roll.

"Hell, you're right." Barber smiled and he almost looked human. He almost looked Italian. "I'll vote for your friend."

"I'd personally appreciate it."

"But next thing you know, they'll be letting *broads* in. Then it'll really be the pits around here."

That left me to wonder what sort of creature he was going home to. But we finished the game without further conversation.

This was an early night for most members, and by the time I had finished my workout, there was only one other man in the shower room. I heard his spray and the sound of grunting and lathering as I moved in for a quick drench and out again.

I was already dried off, combed, and pulling on my dainties when I met with the other straggler.

A breathtaking young lion clad only in a towel limped into the locker room, bent almost double. He gingerly sat on the bench, digging his right fist into his back, then glanced up at me and tossed his dripping blond mane.

He smiled through tears; his teeth were as perfect as the rest of him.

"You have to be Matt Sinclair."

"I don't have to be; I want to be."

"So do I, I think." He heaved his magnificently furred chest in a pained sigh and held out his hand. "Right now I'd rather be anyone but Bill Oakes."

I shook the hand firmly, resisting an impulse to kneel and kiss it.

"*Enchanté,* Mr. Oakes."

I don't know what it is about me and football linemen. Their proximity alone raises my blood pressure and causes my heart to pound. But outwardly I stayed cool.

"Just Bill." He clutched at his back again and winced. "Nineteen seventy-six. One of my own team mates cut-blocked me at scrimmage and put me on the bench for five Sundays. Every once in a while I throw the damn thing out again. Can't move. Like now. I may have to get four strong men to carry me out of here."

"Try chiropractic?"

"Yeah, I have to go almost every week. I should get the guy to live in."

"I can unjam it for you, if you don't mind an enthusiastic amateur."

"You kidding?"

"No."

He looked me up and down. "I'll pass."

"Suit yourself." I pulled on my trousers to decarnalize my impression. "Through none of my own doing, it seems that I've become involved in the passing of your partner, Brad Rutleldge."

"Yeah? Me, too."

I pulled my socks up and reached for my wingtip oxfords. "If we solve the mystery surrounding his death, maybe we can both get uninvolved."

"I'm for that."

"Will you give me a few facts about the man?"

"If I can. Brad and I were in business together, but I don't think I knew him at all." This was grunted out. The delicious hunk was still in too much pain to attempt dressing and remained bent over.

"Did you know he had an option on some of Eisenhardt's property?"

Bill gritted his teeth. "I sure as hell didn't. Two years ago, I offered the Cowboy half a million for that small northern parcel he wasn't even using, and he nearly spit tobacco juice in my face. Said he'd never sell."

"Apparently Brad offered considerably more."

"I'd like to know what. I'd also like to have that option in my hands. We could do a great subdivision out there." Bill was digging his fist into his back. It wasn't working.

"If the option belongs to the partnership, it's yours already."

"Who says he bought it for the partnership? Brad might have done some promoting on his own."

I perched on the massage table to lace my shoes.

"Was he in the habit of making deals behind your back?"

"Listen, treachery was his middle name. I was going to dissolve the corporation and get my money out after this casino deal." There was a grimace and he bit back a groan.

"Suppose you found no money left in?"

"Come again?"

"Happy to. What if Brad siphoned off the money from your partnership to make his own little investments on the side? Like the Eisenhardt land?"

"Highly illegal."

"A clever accountant can show paper losses in the partnership and paper gains in his personal enterprises."

"I guess he can. And Brad was clever. Give him that."

"Okay, let's get to the next stage. Did Frank Washington visit you yet?"

"Bet on it. The wife is usually the first suspect, but Brad was a bachelor, so the partner is next. Not that I had much to tell him."

"Did Frank happen to toss you a hank of rope and—?"

"Yes." He interrupted with the impatience of a man in pain. "I can tie a slip bowline or any other knot you care to name. I used to be an Eagle Scout."

"One might say you had the most to gain from the murder."

"One might."

"And also point out that you would have access to the victim's house. And even that you're a big strong brute of a man and no stranger to violence."

"I was an offensive lineman. I broke bones for a living."

"And you could have hanged a shrimp like Brad without a gibbet. Just held him out at arm's length while he bounced and kicked."

"Right this minute I couldn't hold up a woman's skirt. You have a vivid imagination."

"Then I'll imagine that you met Brad and learned that he had used your money to buy himself an option on Cowboy's property. Imagine you got in a rage, and the old 'sack the quarterback' spirit took over."

Bill shook some drops of water from his hair. "So you really think I could have killed him, brute that I am?" He rose slowly, without unbending his back. "You could be dangerous, you know." He did a Hunchback of Notre Dame impression over to the table and momentarily looked down at me, grinding his teeth and flexing the muscles of his right arm. I could almost feel the strength rippling through it, enough strength to punch my head against the far wall and give it some english.

"Okay, Matt."

He rewrapped the towel carefully and lay belly down on the massage table. "Do what you can about this pain."

"My pleasure."

I'm a tutored amateur, having shared quarters with a chiropractor some fifteen years ago. During that time, the profession wasn't legally recognized here in Louisiana, and its practitioners were status-rated somewhere between fortune tellers and back alley abortionists. But after seeing some hundred furtive patients stagger into my friend's office and march out, I gained respect for the discipline.

I ran my thumbs down Bill's spine to ascertain the trouble spot. It was a most common sports injury, the first lumbar vertebra out of alignment to the right.

"Some laterality in your L-one."

"That's what everyone says," he told the floor tiles.

"Mind a double-thenar maneuver? It's pretty rough."

"Either that or shoot me."

"You asked for it." I opened my palms to expose the bony prominences beneath my thumbs and hooked them underneath the lumbar vertebra. Then I locked my elbows and lunged headward with all my hundred and fifty-five pounds, till a loud cracking sound echoed off the tile walls as the vertebra unhinged.

Bill's groan was muffled as he bit into the back of his hand.

After a few seconds, he caught his breath again and said, "Thanks. That did it."

"A little massage will help you feel better."

He lifted his muscular shoulders, then let them drop.

"Go ahead. I'm compromised already."

In a few moments, under my ministrations, his tension abated and he closed his eyes.

I said, "Edwina Devon told me about you."

"Me, too." His answer was tired and sad. "I'm in love with that woman, you know. I'd marry her in a New York second, but she'd rather have you. Can you figure that?"

"Not when she can have *you*. No indeed."

I dug my palms into his shoulders to alleviate the stiffness, then moved down to his deltoids. By now I had to stand seven inches away from the table.

"She's beautiful, Matt. Delicate, refined. I adore her, really."

"I understand."

No, I didn't.

Why was he burbling on so about a mere female when *I* could have made his ears ring?

"You know what?" His eyes were closed, his voice wistful. "She says you're a better lover than I am. And here you are a fru— gay person."

"Maybe that's why it's easier for me to make love to a female. Because I never get carried away, I can be scientific about it. A man must seem to be in control."

"Seem to be?"

"A woman expects you to take absolute command of the lovemaking. But then you're supposed to use that power to give her exactly what she wants."

"God knows, I try hard enough. But dammit, she never tells me what the hell she wants. Am I supposed to be a mind reader or something?"

"Exactly, Bill." I ran my hands over the knotted muscles of his biceps. "Prince Charming is supposed to intuit Snow White's every desire and fulfill it grandly. That's part of the game."

"How do I do that?"

"In the absence of clues, just assume she wants the whole bleedin' worship service. Begin at her left ear and work your way down." Now I was working my own way down his back, doing shiatsu alongside his spinal column. "Edwina is very sensitive around the pulse point of her throat, so stop there for twenty seconds.

Then you caress her breasts, making circles around her nipples with your palms so they get good and hard."

"Good and hard. Yes. Oh lordy!"

I retained the tenor of a medical school lecture.

"Keep to the same rhythm as her heartbeat while you get some strong contractions going. When she starts snapping her head back with each stroke, that's the signal to press on."

"Yeah?" Now Bill's hair was standing on the back of his neck. "Then what should I do?"

"To achieve the optimum clitoral stimulation, you might set the female on your lap with her back against you. Then reach around her for maximum control."

"I might . . . yeah."

I dug my hands into the flesh of his midsection hard enough to hurt then let go.

"Wrap your left arm around and squeeze her right breast. Then with just the first two fingers of your right, gently hold her labia minora together and massage her langette between them."

The back of his neck was sweating, so I blew on it to cool him. "That's extremely delicate, so you mustn't touch it directly with anything but your tongue."

"Ooh, yeah . . . My tongue."

"And while you're doing that, use your index finger to determine the stage of lubrication."

"Yeah. Right."

"When Edwina spreads her legs wide and makes little moaning noises, that's the go signal. So give it to her forthrightly in a steady beat." Bill's breathing had quickened till he was nearly rasping. "Try . . . oh . . . four shallow strokes to one deep. After about two minutes of that you see her nipples pucker, she digs her nails into your arms, and a rosy flush appears all over her midriff. Then when she screams—"

"Oh shit!"

"—when she screams, you'll know you've brought her to the top . . . but you're not finished yet. That's when she's ballooning. Her *galette* just sucks you in and she wants it really hard." Bill arched his back and gripped the sides of the table as I worked the tightness out of his gluteus. "So pull her ankles up and give it all you've got."

"Wait! All I've got is *gone*."

"Try doing multiplication tables in base five—whatever works. I figure discounts on season closeouts. Anyhow, when she stops writhing and just sort of lies still and sobs, then you'll know she's fully satisfied and you can let go."

Bill grunted like a boar hog and went limp.

"You make it sound possible if not easy. I'm grateful for the advice and I'll live by it."

"Anything to bring you lovebirds together. Call me Cupid."

"I'll call you something, all right."

Chapter 11
Friday Morning, March 10th

I was checking my ad copy for *New Orleans* magazine when Steve Hicks leaned into the office and whistled.

"Do you want to see a dude named Bill Oakes? Tall, blond, sort o' muscular?"

I popped right up. "Steve, when you see anything looking that good, you don't have to ask. Just send him in."

"How am I supposed to know what you consider good? To me, *Charo* looks good."

"You're fired."

Bill carried in a Vuitton briefcase and set it on my desk before shaking hands. His blue three-piece suit was custom tailored of a fine light wool, but still it seemed not to fit him. Linemen always look awkward and musclebound in a suit . . . though delicious without one.

I stifled a swoon and invited him to sit down, but he shook his magnificent head.

"I really don't have time. Listen, Matt, I was clearing out my partner's trash this morning." He opened his briefcase. "And when I found this paper with your name on it, I brought it right over, seeing as you were straight with me."

"Pardon?"

"Hell, you know what I mean." He riffled through a sheaf of notes and extracted a tattered photocopy. "This may have been what Brad showed you the morning **before he died.**"

I recognized the form from my days of genealogy research.

"This is a page from the microfilmed archives, a census record from eighteen twenty. What could it have to do with me?"

"I can't imagine. But look at that penciled note in the margin: 'Coulet-Mouton-Vigé-Sinclair.' "

I moved my finger down the page and stopped it at the name Coulet. In the household of one Bernard du Bois were counted a free mulatto maid, Aglae Coulet, and her two daughters; Catherine and Therese. The girls were quadroons. Coulet-Mouton-Vigé? My gut turned.

Bill replaced the other papers and locked his briefcase.

"Does that mean anything to you? Does it help?"

I laughed to keep from crying. "My friend, you may have helped me right into a bad case of nerves."

"I'm sorry. I thought you could use it."

"You were right. This information is vital. And I'm grateful, Bill."

"Good." Then he clasped his ham hands and looked embarrassed. "Would you do something for me now?"

I sprang up. "*Would* I! Anything you can name, you great tawny beast."

He blushed. "Nothing like that. I meant . . . would you sort of put in a word for me with Edwina? You don't really want her for yourself, do you? That would be impossible. But she respects your opinion."

"What do you want me to tell her?"

"Just that I love her." It was an act of stark desperation for him to ask this, especially of the likes of me. I didn't doubt that he loved her hopelessly. "And maybe that I'm not such a lout. Please?"

"I'll speak for you, Bill. But remember what happened to Miles Standish."

After dispatching him with more thanks, I called Steve back.

He winked as he closed the door behind him. "What

went on in here, Matty? Was that big dude one of your many conquests?"

"Don't be silly. You could see that he's straight."

"Yeah, but straight's the way you like 'em. More of a challenge there, right?"

"Not for the challenge. It's just more normal somehow. If I want a man, I'd prefer a real one, not just another fruit."

"In the light of that intelligence, I guess I should be grateful that you never hit on me."

"Go look in the mirror, Steve. You're not exactly a hunk. In fact, that's why I let you work for me. No distraction."

He looked in the wall mirror to frown at his pale, flabby visage and receding hair line.

"What the hell. I still got my personality."

"Anyhow, Bill just dropped by to tell me I was getting screwed—but not in a good way. Do you have Lilly Coleman's invoice?"

"Coming right up." It took him thirty seconds to locate it in the C-D file. "What for?"

"I need her phone number."

"You got it." Steve punched the number in three seconds and handed me the receiver.

Mrs. Coleman's hello was deep and resonant.

"Hello, Miss Lilly. This is Matt Sinclair."

"Well, good mornin', Mister Matt. That new dresser looks just fine in my bedroom. Hey, you're not calling to take it back, are you?"

"No, ma'am. I just wanted to ask you about the candy you left me."

"That?" She chuckled. "It's what you said you wanted."

"When did I say that?"

"When you were first comin' out of your seizure. You kept mumbling something about a mint, so I brought one by. Of course, you wouldn't remember now."

"Thank you, Miss Lilly!" I gushed some further expression of gratitude, said good-bye and grabbed my polo coat. "Steve, send her that Tiffany table lamp as a lagniappe."

"A lagniappe? But we've already lost money on that lady. Hey, where are you going?"

"Where I must have been going the morning Brad died. To the Old Mint!"

It was with the worst of wills that I followed Clark Fidey through the French Market as he plied his art. He stopped in the first stall under the cement archway and turned a mushroom over critically.

"This looks a little wilted, Ben. I sure would appreciate it if you would throw it in gratis."

Poor Ben shrugged assent, and Fidey added this new trophy to a shopping bag scored from Kreeger's. When I had agreed to join him in "making groceries," I hadn't realized how embarrassing it would be to accompany someone who tries to mooch as much as he buys. But I needed his expertise, so I just turned my head and pretended not to know him as he worked his way among the tables of produce, assembling his salad or vegetable soup.

I used real cash money to buy some especially gorgeous hot green peppers. Fidey shook his ratty head at them. (He must have cut his hair himself under a low-watt bulb with dull scissors.)

"Can't eat those things. My ulcers."

"You've had ulcers ever since I met you. They can be cured with surgery, you know."

"Do you have any idea what surgeons charge these days? Not to mention nurses and hospitals. I'll just take my Maalox."

"If an operation is necessary, your insurance will cover most of it."

"Do you know what insurance companies charge these days?"

"Suit yourself.—What about my problem? Is it possible we may still have a good title?"

"Indisputably. What you think you want is proof that there was some mistake, right? Maybe that ancestor of yours, Emelie Mouton, didn't have Negro blood." The issue was Louisiana's inheritance laws, which were circumscribed by racial qualifications throughout most of the nineteenth century.

"Or maybe she and Francis Vigé reaffirmed their marriage vows ten years later, when it would have been legal."

"That's possible. Some couples would get hitched in a civil ceremony because there was no priest available. Then they would have it blessed months or years later. In that case it would have been legal."

"I'll take that."

"But . . ." He held up a brown banana. The vendor waved and he added it to his collection bag. "But that would only happen out in some rural parishes. Here in New Orleans, there was always a priest around. Indisputably."

"Well, suppose they got married in some jurisdiction where miscegenation wasn't against the law."

"Where? Louisiana was the most liberal territory in the deep South. You think maybe your ancestors got on a plane and flew off to New York or the Caribbean?"

"What if they got married on the high seas by a ship's captain?"

"Slave ship?" He laughed. A lot because oxygen is free.

I said, "It will serve me as well if you can discover that Emelie Mouton was less than one-eighth Negro."

"If the woman had even one-sixteenth traceable African blood, then she was legally black in this state." He found a twig of grapes on the cement floor and claimed it. "If there is some way around your problem in the records, I'm the man to find it. Indisputably. Let's walk over to my house, and I'll write down your names and dates. As much as you've got."

The first person possessive pronoun was oratorical license. "His" house actually belonged to his mother, Abbie Fuller Fidey, a distant cousin of mine who was heiress to a real estate fortune back before the Depression. Now she owned nothing but her once grand classic-style townhouse on Royal Street. She was forcibly retired from her position as the oldest lingerie clerk in New Orleans when the Common Street branch of Sears was forced to close its doors last year. Now all that remained between her and glory was a minuscule Social Security check.

And Clark was probably the oldest man in New Orleans never to have supported himself.

As we trod the disintegrating flagstones of the front walk, I stopped to admire the denticulated parapet above the Corinthian columns on the second story. And then I caught sight of the lady of the house on her knees in the side yard, slashing feebly through a fairy ring of fungus with a sickle. I moved to help her, but Fidey caught my arm.

"Only exercise she gets, my mom. Gardening is good for her. Indisputably."

Mrs. Fidey rocked back on her heels, panting, and shook dried leaves out of her gossamer-fine white hair, seeming to have left off her "healthful exercise" for the moment. So I was able to turn my back on the woman and follow her devoted son across the paint-chipped front gallery and into the house. The inside was even more neglected than its facade, the parlor looking as though construction work had been started and long abandoned. Plaster was flaking off the walls and had been replaced sporadically with sheet rock. Canvas tarps covered most of the floor and some of the faded and sagging furniture. Sawhorses held a plank for a make-shift coffee table, and a gray layer of dust covered everything in sight.

Stepping over a disassembled mantelpiece, I imagined how depressing this disorder would be to a lady of Mrs. Fidey's sensibilities and said so.

"She's used to it," my host breezed as he led me into the shambles of a kitchen. He uncapped his pen and scrawled "CLARK" across his bag of vegetables before storing it in the refrigerator. "Mom is very honest, but if I don't do this, she might forget and eat some. Then I'd have to feel like some kind of cheapskate asking her for the money."

"I should imagine that you would."

"She's lucky I live here, what with the crime situation the way it is." He beckoned me to accompany him up the footworn, creaking stairs to the second floor. "What would she do without me?"

"I wonder." I looked down the gloomy hallway through the door of the first bedroom. This was obviously the mother's, because cotton frocks hung in the alcove where a closet should have been. Layers of wallpaper from a dozen different eras were peeling in strips. The molding had come loose from the ceiling, and the only electrical outlet was a single overhead fixture with a spider of wires dropping therefrom. One corner of the bed was propped up on a cement block.

The room had been swept and dusted, but still it looked like the set of a Tennesee Williams play.

Clark used his key on the second door and, with a proprietory wave, invited me to enter.

Having expected the same sort of blight I'd seen up till now, I caught my breath at the taste and elegance displayed here. All the furnishings were real Victorian antiques in mint condition and polished with lemon oil. The wallpaper was new but of a design appropriate to the mid-nineteenth century, and the draperies and bed canopy were a fine velvet.

My eyes locked on the oil painting over the gilded secretaire. It was a Biblical scene in the style of the

Pre-Raphaelite revivalists. The figures were pale and languid.

"Is this a real Rossetti?!"

Fidey folded his arms and lifted his chin in pride.

"Indisputably."

Gabriel Dante Rossetti's sentimental classicism has long been out of favor, but he was all the rage during the latter Victorian era. And this painting very much belonged on this wall in this setting.

I feasted my eyes for several moments, picking up a Stourbridge *millefiori* paperweight.

"These furnishings are incredible! Why don't you do the whole house like this?"

"No need, Matt. I spend all my time in this room here." Fidey hung his coat on a mahogany valet. "I maintain the structural integrity of the place, shore it up, keep the roof tight—just what's necessary." He bade me sit on the museum quality prie-dieu chair with cabriole legs, painted and inlaid with mother-of-pearl. I did so gingerly. "I've studied every book I could find on Victoriana, and I'm going to restore this house to exactly what it might have looked like in eighteen sixty-two. I've saved all the original cornices and medallions. Did you see that mantelpiece on the floor downstairs? Well, that's going to be sanded down and painted so that all the original relief shows."

"Very ambitious."

He ran his hand along the carving on a balloon-back drawing room chair. "I'm going to put everything I have into this house. It will be worth five hundred thousand, exclusive of furnishings by the time I get through. I'll have the showcase of Marigny. That's what they called this house when Mom was growing up here. I'll get into the *Dixie Roto*, too. Just you wait."

"Wait for what?"

"Until Mom passes away. Then I'll call the contractors in."

"You won't make any improvements until the house is yours, is that it?"

His door was still slightly ajar, and I glimpsed Mrs. Fidey peering in at us, blinking birdlike over a handful of garden cuttings. Clark casually closed the door, leaving her on the outside, and seated himself at the secretaire. He opened the top drawer for his Maalox and took a swig before getting down to business.

"What you want will date back before the War Between the States." He checked his watch. "Lunch hour is over. Soon as I get back to the Mint, I'll go into the black boxes. Check records from St. Louis Cathedral as well as all the legal ones. I'll get you photocopies clear as the originals."

"All I need is something readable. And provable in court."

Chapter 12
Friday Afternoon, March 10th

He came up behind me on my way home from Clark's, and I smelled his Version Originale before I felt his hand on my shoulder. Lawrence Dale looked solemn.

"Matty, you'll have to come with me."

"Have to?"

"Have to." He waved at a black Cadillac limousine parked ten feet away at the bus stop. Traffic laws didn't apply to these people.

Theoretically, I could have resisted—run down Royal Street screaming for all I was worth. He wouldn't have galloped through the crowd after me, hollering and shooting. But in the long view there was no fighting it. So I smiled right back at him as though he were inviting me for a cuddle.

"Where to, Lawrence?"

He opened the rear door for me. "The Roosevelt."

The Roosevelt is the oldest luxury hotel in New Orleans. The Fairmont people have long owned and renamed it, but to us natives it will always be the Roosevelt.

We walked through the entranceway, passing the doorman, resplendent in gold braid, and trod the oriental-style carpeting through the lobby. Lawrence veered left and stepped ahead of me to press the elevator button. Our destination was a double suite on the top floor, at the top rate.

Two primates in need of a shave sat in the front room like sleepy guard dogs. Relaxing among loved ones, they didn't have to impress anyone with their degree of civilization. So they sprawled in their shirt-sleeves with shoulder holsters in plain view. Lawrence pointed me ahead to the central parlor, where I was to be allowed an audience with Thomas Sacci himself.

The all-powerful don appeared to be about sixty years old; he was not much over five feet tall and had very little hair, combed in long strands over his pate. This unprepossessing package was expensively wrapped in a double-breasted, gray pin-striped suit by Redaelli, a white-on-white shirt, and hand-painted tie. He was seated, or rather enthroned, in a gilded cathedral chair piled so high with cushions that he sat nearly at eye level with a standing man. He waved us forward with a soft, manicured hand, and Lawrence approached him as reverently as a kid going to meet Santa.

I didn't know whether I was expected to kiss Sacci's hand as Lawrence had. But then I decided he wouldn't want me to fog up the four-carat stone on his pinky ring, so settled for a bow.

We had not had an official godfather in New Orleans since Chico Manguno died in prison the year before. Various of his lieutenants were vying for the position, and eventually whoever had not given up or been blown up by the time the dust cleared would be anointed. Sacci, the *capo* from Las Vegas, perhaps had come to town to lend his support to one faction or another.

Were I in the contest, I decided, I'd listen to his advice.

I tore my eyes away from him and glanced around the suite. The only untidy note was a large steamer trunk that had been unpacked and left to stand empty. It was a fine-looking trunk in black leather with brass fittings, but for some reason I didn't like it.

I took the chair Lawrence indicated, which was un-comfortably lowslung.

"I am aware of your enormous influence, Mr. Sacci. I ask nothing of you and fervently hope that you ask nothing of me."

"My organization doesn't want something for nothing, Sinclair. I know you're legitimate and you don't owe us anything." Now that I was safely seated, he pulled himself out of his chair so he could walk over and be taller than I. "But there are other interests that have intruded themselves and we have to protect our position." He jerked a thumb at Lawrence. "Get him whatever he drinks."

The delectable young button man didn't ask for my order but just moved to the bar, poured two jiggers of Wild Turkey into a glass of ice, and felt around for the Abisante.

"I've never stepped on your toes," I said.

"No, it's your riverfront land we have to discuss. Some business rivals of ours have already made a proposition to you regarding that property."

"Which I turned down."

"But they were very insistent, I hear."

"They were."

"So DiMarco saved your ass one time. But he can't always be handy, right? Next time you might crumble. Sell out. Who could blame you?"

"That land stays in my family."

"You got whaddaya call 'dynastic pretensions'? Looking to the future generations?" He swaggered around the perimeter of the rug, orating to the draperies. "Guess that's natural for a man. Even your kind. Sure, you want to live a long time and have children and grandchildren. Used to be a guy could count on that, you know? But this is a difficult age we're in. Foreign terrorists." He smiled. "Domestic terrorists. Unhappy friends. DiMarco, even you could be an unhappy friend and kill Mr. Sinclair, couldn't you?"

Lawrence put his head down.

"On your order, *signore*. But not for money." He twisted a lemon peel over the top of the Sazerac and brought it to me, then hovered deferentially while I sipped his effort. It was perfect and I said so.

"How about that?" Sacci rubbed his hands together. "He likes you. DiMarco there is a *finocchio*, but he's a good man just the same. Totally loyal. All my men defer to my judgment."

He strode over to the open trunk and swept his hand around inside it in the manner of a stage magician demonstrating that it was empty.

"This could hold an awful lot. And we intend to pack it ourselves. Won't bother the bellman. Know what I mean?"

"I think I get it."

"You don't have to be a psychic or anything. Just so we understand each other. And we get peace of mind, both of us. Nobody is hurt, right?"

"I understand very well."

"Then let's all be perfectly fair with each other. How about selling me that riverfront property at one hundred fifty percent of current market. Right here and now."

"No, Mr. Sacci, I will not sell that land to you or anyone else. It stays in my family."

"That your last word?"

"Absolutely."

"Too bad, but I was prepared for you to be stubborn." Sacci glanced over at the two primates, who met his gaze eagerly. They were bored and would welcome a little murderous action. But then he turned away from them. "DiMarco?"

"I'm truly sorry, Matty."

Lawrence bent one knee and liberated the twenty-two automatic from his ankle holster, a perfect indoor pistol. It wouldn't make too loud a noise or blow too big a hole. To this he attached a silencer from his coat pocket. His face showed no expression throughout the procedure, but I could see he'd lost color. This was probably only a result of his intense concentration and the same every time. It was not for me to be flattered.

I stood up and knocked back the Sazerac to anesthetize. Then Lawrence took the empty glass from me and set it down neatly before seeing to the grimmer business.

He gripped the back of my neck; his voice was robotic.

"Kneel down. It's easier that way. Really."

I'm bigger and stronger than he is and could have put up a fight just to show whose side I was on, but that macho gesture would only have got me pummeled into the carpet by the guard dogs. So I went to both knees and clasped my hands in front of me—not to pray, but to keep them from shaking. Trunk or no, I had decided that the drama was all bluff. A *capo* with Sacci's high visibility and prestige was not going to have a local merchant bumped off in his hotel suite and then carted downstairs through the lobby in a steamer trunk. This simply is not the way business is conducted in the 1980s.

But apparently Lawrence hadn't been let in on the joke, because I felt his tension in the barrel of his silencer, which nestled in the curly hair at the base of my skull. He stood two feet away from me and held the gun at arm's length as he cocked it. A loyal family man.

"On your order, *signore*," he said again softly.

I heard an intake of breath. Preparatory to a command?

"I ask you for the last time, Sinclair. Will you sell me that land?"

"Whatever you do to me, that stays in my family."

I stared at the rug until the pattern swam and blurred. If I had miscalculated the *capo*'s intentions, I would never know it. But I shut my eyes anyway, because I didn't want to be there when it happened.

Having about five seconds to contemplate whether those brave words would be my epitaph, I could be confident only that Lawrence was a professional and that his finger wouldn't reflexively tighten on the trigger and send me to hell before the order was given.

It wasn't given. Instead, Sacci must have spared my life with some gesture that I couldn't see, because I felt all the tension leave Lawrence's body, though he did nothing but point the weapon away from me, carefully uncock it, and detach the silencer.

It was left to Sacci to say, "Awright, brave man. You can get up now."

Lawrence put a hand out to help me to my feet and I took it. (What the heck.)

The *capo* had been enjoying our exercise from a lounging posture on his throne. "You seem pretty strong-headed on the subject of real estate."

"It's like this, sir. I'm aware that you could kill me." I brushed a thread of lint off my knee. "But if I were to sell her favorite parcel of land, my *mother* would kill me, and I would rather you than she. Because I'm almost certain that she would be upset afterward."

"Yeah? I got a mother, too. And she almost killed me a few times." He laughed with his mouth only. "But my thinking is, if you won't sell to me, even with a gun to your head, then there's no way you'll sell to my competitors either."

"You may be assured of that, Mr. Sacci."

"DiMarco? Take him home."

"Yes, sir."

Lawrence opened the door of the suite for me. Once in the corridor though, he didn't lead me straight to the elevator but stopped halfway instead and shoved open the door to the fire stairs. Then he jerked me through it so quickly that the sudden violence of the move took me completely by surprise. He kicked the heavy door closed behind us and shoved me against the wall hard enough that my head bounced.

"*Pazzo!* Are you crazy!? Who the fuck ya think yer *dealin'* wit' here!?"

I'd known Lawrence was Italian but had never before seen him show so much emotion. Except in bed.

The lad's hard-won prep school elocution had evaporated in the heat of the moment, and he'd reverted to his native tongue, the staccato dialect of Chicago's Little Italy. So too had gone his veneer of WASP cool. He waved his hands frantically in front of my face as though beating back a swarm of gnats.

" 'Ey! Whatsit? 'Ey!"

Fortunately, the Sinclairs have been in this country too long to get excited about anything, so I was able to keep my calm.

"I've heard about Thomas Sacci."

"Then what're you? Suicidal? You came within one inch of gettin' blown away back there! And *me*! I would have had to *do* it!"

His green eyes were burning. I gripped his shoulders.

"Relax, boy. Couldn't you see it was only a bluff?"

"A bluff?" All the breath had left him and this just squeaked out. "Is that what you thought? My God!" I let go of his shoulders because they were trembling so. "I've known Sacci since I was fifteen. That's ten years. And I had to help carry those fuckin' trunks downstairs more than one time. He was not bluffing, Matty!"

Now my knees unlocked. I slid down the wall till I landed on my butt with a thump. "But I'm still alive."

"You're alive because he changed his mind at the last minute. He actually had his hand up to give me the order. But then I saw the sequence of thought go through his eyes: He figured that if you'd rather die than sell, he could let the opposition take you out. You protect our position and we save a six hundred dollar trunk. Sacci is an animal, Matty. Don't have any delusions about the 'New Mafia' and legitimate enterprises." Lawrence put his hand out to help me up for the second time in five minutes. "He got to the top the same way as any other don. By shooting widows and orphans in the back."

"So why do you work for him?"

"What are you? The Milton Berle of New Orleans? I'm not a free agent. This is just like at Angola. I never had the luxury of marrying for love."

"You chose your way of life."

"Yeah, and there were so many opportunities for a kid like me. I could've been a hairdresser back in Chicago. Maybe a female impersonator."

"You're smart. You could have been anything."

"So, I took a shortcut, all right? I'm not complaining either. I'm just telling you the way it is." He grabbed my tie and stood up on his toes, butting my forehead. "And this is the way it is. When Thomas Sacci says, 'Shit!,' *you* say, 'How many pounds and what color?' Get it?"

"Pounds and color. Well, I understand, but—"

"That way you get to live!"

"You're overlooking one salient factor, sweetums. I'm still more afraid of my mother than I am of Thomas Sacci."

"Your mother? Again with your *mother*! *Madre mia!* You really are a *finocchio*!" He carefully smoothed the knot of my tie, then kissed me hard on the lips. "Now I'll take you home. Just remember you almost didn't get to sit up for this ride."

I felt very grand alighting from the limousine when it pulled up in front of the house. But the pride dissipated quickly when I saw Frank waiting in my living room, Heineken beer in hand. He had seen the car through the window.

"Thomas Sacci is in town," I said weakly.

"I know. So why did you feel it necessary to call on him at the Roosevelt?"

"Just so he could watch Lawrence Dale put me on my knees and hold his favorite gun to my skull. You wouldn't deprive him of a little innocent merriment, would you?"

"Not when you put it that way."

"Since your boys in blue are keeping such a close watch on the Roosevelt, maybe you can do me a favor."

"Sure. What's that?"

"If they see a couple of Sacci's thugs humping a big black steamer trunk out through the lobby, I would like them to stop and check it."

"Fair enough."

"And if they find me inside, I would like you to arrange for a dignified interment in the Sinclair family vault."

"Why not?" He finished his beer. "I thought Lawrence would be an asset to us, but I was kidding myself. I'll have him picked up."

"No, don't do that, Frank. In his own peculiar way, he's on my side."

I heard the phone beep, and Robin came in carrying the receiver. "It's Clark Fidey."

"So soon? Excuse me, Frank." Frank waved assent and I took the receiver. "Yes, Clark?"

"Hey, Matt. I'm calling from the Mint. I got some good news and some bad news about your ancestry."

"You work fast."

"It really only took one document. But just in case you can't figure it out yourself, I wrote down a summary of the facts on this sheet of yellow legal paper I have right in front of me."

"Will it prove my title?"

"Indisputably. I made photocopies of everything relevant to your case and I'm bringing them home. But you've got to pay me first, Matt. I don't give anything away." There was a pause while he took a drink, probably of Maalox. "And I have a feeling that some other people might be interested in this research, too."

"Forget the other people. I'll bring my checkbook."

"Cold cash. I don't believe in taxes."

Chapter 13
Saturday Morning, March 11th

I couldn't fill Clark's demand for "cold cash" until my bank opened. So by the time I arrived at the Fidey home, it was nearly ten thirty. And, lo and behold!, Frank Washington was there ahead of me, standing outside on the banquette.

"What are you doing here, Matt?"

"I came to see Clark. You remember that call I took last night? He phoned to say he has information for me."

"You'll have the devil's own time getting it out of him now. Clark Fidey is dead."

"Dead?"

"Indisputably. He died sometime early this morning."

"I see." And I saw.

Frank leaned over the hood of the blue and white squad car and flipped open his notebook. "This morning, his mother tried to rouse him at the usual time and there was no answer. After a few minutes, she panicked. Fidey had locked the door from the inside, so she had to call for police assistance to break through. The deceased was found curled up on the floor. He hadn't been dead more than a couple of hours."

"How unfortunate."

"Old Mrs. Fidey is still up there. She refuses to leave the room he died in, and my men didn't have the heart to force her out. Poor thing's got nothing left now."

"She had nothing before."

"Physical evidence indicates that the deceased died of massive hemorrhaging of the intestinal tract."

"He did have ulcers."

"This was worse than ulcers, Matt. He must have suffered violent abdominal pains, vomiting, and bloody diarrhea."

"Please! I haven't had breakfast yet."

"I never knew the man too well. Maybe you can tell me why he didn't call 911 for an ambulance when all these symptoms started."

"Ask anyone about Fidey." The shade of his bedroom window was up, and I could discern the silhouette of a sitting woman. "He hated to spend money on health care. He's had ulcers for a long time and must have thought he could just take some Maalox, as usual, and wait out the cramps."

"I see. By the time he realized it was serious, he might have been too far gone to make the call." Frank made a brief note to that effect. "Never mind the ulcers, though. We suspect the deceased died of food poisoning." He closed the notebook with a bang. "We'll just get the Orleans Parish coroner to put down his trumpet and do an autopsy."

Frank climbed into his seat behind the "To Protect and to Serve" fiction and conscientiously fastened his seat belt as his rookie drove him away. But two cop cars remained to guard the death scene. I tried my luck in the house anyway.

Duffy was leaning against the front door jamb making jokes appropriate to the occasion.

"Whatchu doin', Matt? You wouldn't want to disturb the forensic evidence?"

"I'd just like to go upstairs and comfort Mrs. Fidey, if you don't mind."

"Can't hurt. But I warn you, it doesn't smell too good up there."

Abbie Fuller Fidey was huddled up in the balloon-back chair, keeping her feet out of the filth on the rug, inside the taped outline of her late son.

She gazed dreamily at the Rossetti painting and

seemed not to note my presence until I touched her arm.

"Miss Abbie? Do you remember me?"

She turned around as slowly as Norman Bates's mother in the fruit cellar and didn't look much better.

"Remember? Of course I do. You're Clementine's boy, little Matty."

"Yes. Matt Sinclair."

"You're very good to your mother, too. She told me that when we had tea last week." Her voice was far away. Perhaps the medical examiner had given her something to calm her in her grief.

She hadn't taken tea with my mother in decades.

I said, "I agreed to pay Clark for some documents. But if they're here, I can pay you instead."

"Pay me?" She made a faint little laughing sound. "That would be nice. Indeed it would. He brought quite a batch of them home from the Mint." A clawlike hand pointed. "There in the desk. What do you make of them?"

I opened the secretaire and found there a bale of photocopies. Census information, records of baptisms, marriages, births, and deaths. Deeds and court notices. Endless lists of names of New Orleanians who had been dead for generations, names that still live on in their local descendants. I quickly shuffled through the pile, not finding what I'd come for.

"But there was a summary of his conclusions. Clark said he wrote it on a sheet of yellow legal paper."

"A yellow paper. No, you can't have that one."

"I can't?"

"Because you see," Mrs. Fidey showed her gnarled palms. "The yellow paper isn't here."

I watched my feet, keeping them out of the muck, and squatted in front of her.

"How could it not be here?"

"Because"—she looked coquettish and confidential—"he sold that one already to another gentleman."

"I talked to your son last night."

She bobbed her head. "That's right. It was last night. Last night my son sold some very important research paper. About the Vigé-Sinclair title, he said." She caressed the intricate carving on her chair. "I knew your father, Arthur, quite well. How dashing he looked at my debut, in his Army Air Force uniform. Oh, and such a fine dancer."

"Yes, he was." I took a deep breath and made my voice gentle. "Listen, Miss Abbie. Did someone come to the house to buy that paper?"

"He certainly did for 'cold cash.' Clark always insists on 'cold cash.' My son is very smart."

"I know."

"You see how he restored my house? It's just the way it used to be when I was a girl. Soon I'll be entertaining again."

"Yes, ma'am."

"The parlor downstairs is lovely again. Elegant. Did you see?"

"I saw it." I had just passed through the parlor, again dodging around dust, powdered plaster, and fallen moldings. Only in this room was the old woman able to fantasize and recapture the splendor of her girlhood.

"I must have Clementine over for tea. Perhaps next week."

"Yes, ma'am. Can you remember at all who paid Clark for that yellow paper?"

"Not his name. Not that. But he was so very nice to me. Charming and polite." She tapped my shoulder with a long and yellow fingernail. "Hardly anyone takes the time to be polite these days, you know? It's not like when you and I were young and everyone had such fine manners. . . . And how the beaux would gather round then. My dance card was always filled . . ."

Her eyes glistened momentarily then focused back on me. "Do you remember when I was seventeen? And how you held me so tight while we danced? So scandalously tight, Arthur?"

"Yes. I remember."

"Wasn't I pretty then?"

I took her hand in both of mine.

"You were beautiful, Abbie. Like no other girl."

Chapter 14
Saturday Afternoon, March 11th

I had sorted Clark's bundle of photocopies on my desk: French documents in one pile, Spanish in another, English in the third. Legal documents representing the different colonial eras of New Orleans. There have been Vigés here since 1721. And a few of Fidey's odd bills and notices dated farther back than that. But everything was relevent. Fidey thought so, and he was the best of his profession.

Steve Hicks knocked on my open door.

"Herman Gross is outside. He said you would want to see him."

Gross is the most hustling real estate broker on the Delta.

"He lied."

"I'll tell him to go away."

"No. He'll just stand out in the showroom and whine. You'd better let him in."

I swept the photocopies into my desk drawer before rising to welcome the unwelcome with a firm handshake.

"Good afternoon, Herman."

"Good? Don't tell me good. I'm a broken man."

"I'm sorry. Would a drink help fix you?"

"Just maybe a Coke, if it wouldn't be any trouble."

Herman Gross was a vision of shabbiness in a suit that was probably already out of style when he bought it. I suppressed a wince as he lowered his seam-sprung polyester double-knit onto the pure Chinese silk of my office settee. Driven by a spirit of noblesse oblige, I produced his Coke Classic along with a glass of ice. He ignored the glass, then wiped the bottle on his coat sleeve as though suspicious of its origin.

I perched on the edge of my desk. "To what happy circumstance do I owe the honor of this visit?"

"Just wanna schmooz a little. I got a proposition for you."

Business sense dictates that I listen to such propositions.

Two years ago, Gross bought one of the finest old buildings on Esplanade, slapped on a coat of paint and a ten-year roof and apportioned it into fifteen Lilliputian residential units. He could have realized a four hundred percent return on his investment by selling them as condo apartments. But that wasn't enough. So he met with lawyers and city councilmen and came up with a way to make the most obscene profit possible from the enterprise. The answer was, naturally, time-share condos. In this plan, Mr. and Mrs. John Q. Yankee put out a ridiculous amount of capital plus mainte-nance to buy two weeks out of the year in a one-bedroom apartment in glamorous New Orleans—the second two weeks in March, for example. The proud buyers get ripped off because they will tire of this arrangement within the first year. The neighborhood gets ripped off because interested permanent residents are moved out in favor of transients. The hotels and restaurants get ripped off because the Yankees sleep in this dreadful apartment and eat in its teeny kitchen.

But Herman Gross is happy as a pig in slop.

And, theoretically at least, I'm happy, too, because I get to sell him the furnishings for his disgusting little rabbit warrens.

"Are you buying more furniture to make cramped, badly constructed apartments look elegant?"

"Not furniture today. I'm buying something much bigger."

He took out a handkerchief and patted the space under his collar where most other people have a neck.

"I'm gonna do you a favor. You'll be kissin' me when I walk outta here."

"No!"

"Would I lie? Just give a listen. It can't hurt, right?"

Mr. Gross's lack of comeliness seems not to be a detriment, because hardly anyone looks at him. A salesman's voice is his fortune and Gross's is low-pitched and beautifully modulated with a warm Yiddish cadence. He uses this remarkable instrument to beguile, wheedle, cajole, and convince almost anybody of nearly anything.

It's said of Herman Gross that he made his investment capital selling snake oil. Maybe back to the snakes.

I don't know him socially, but I've heard that Herman is a devoted family man, hustling eighteen hours a day to provide his household with more material goods than the average Middle Eastern despot.

I don't think such a poor specimen of his race should be allowed to reproduce, but this man has two daughters, both named after movie stars in accordance with the custom of his people. The girls are lucky enough to take after their mother, but that may be only because they share the same cosmetic surgeon.

"You didn't come here to talk about our riverfront property by any chance?"

He looked alarmed. "Who told you?"

"For some reason, that particular strip of dirt and shells has been on everybody's mind."

"Yeah, I know you got some offers. It used to real popular."

"Used to be?"

"Past tense." He flailed his left hand. "That was when you Sinclairs owned it for sure."

"We don't own it for sure?"

"Word gets around." He leered, showing a set of teeth that could eat corn through a barbed wire fence. "Your family may not have clear title."

"We may not. That's true."

"So me, I'm gonna take a gamble on you. Is that

fair?" He emptied the bottle with a glug-glugging sound.
I offered another Coke but he waved it away. "Can't
take any more carbonation. I lose control. . . . So whether
your title is good or not, I'm willing to pay you for it.
Am I nice or what?"

"You're extremely nice, Herman. But you must know
that the property in question is in my mother's name
and not mine."

"Yeah, but you have power of attorney; I got my
sources. Which means you can do anything you want
with that piece of land, including plant zucchini. So
you can sell it to me. Get some money out of it for
yourselves. Let me be the schnook. Your mother will
thank you."

"And exactly how much are you willing to pay for my
mother's gratitude?"

"Current market value. Okay, call me a crazy man,
'cause that's what I am."

"Not so crazy. Current market value is a lot less than
that land will be worth in a few years with normal
appreciation. And if the casino goes through, the value
will quadruple."

"Yeah, but what if that lot ain't even yours? If your
title isn't good, then you got *makkes*."

"You're a pretty smart businessman, Herman."

"Thank God, I make a good living."

"My point is that you wouldn't invest . . . uh . . .
makkes if you weren't convinced that our title was good."

"Ah? Maybe not. Somebody might sue me, right? Cover
me with paper. So what? My brother-in-law, Marvin,
he's a lawyer. So let him work. The whole megillah
might take years, and I can collect rent meantime. I try
to make it."

"There's only one thing I can promise, Herman. If I
decide to sell that parcel, I'll let you know before I deal
with anyone else."

He leveraged his bulk into a standing position. "What
can I say, huh? That'll have to hold me awhile."

Then Mr. Gross told me the joke about the priest, the rabbi, and the ham sandwich, shook my hand warmly, and took his leave.

Steve hurried to open the front door for him, then came back to meet me.

"Hey, that's an old joke about the priest, the rabbi, and the ham sandwich—I was eavesdropping." Steve took the fauteuil. "Personalities aside, I'd be tempted by his offer."

"I'm not tempted, but considerably cheered." I rose and dropped Herman's empty bottle into the wastebasket. "Where do you think he found out?"

"About your not having clear title? Gee." He swayed his feet at the puzzle, then drew them up abruptly. "Brad Rutledge told him."

"What for? Brad wanted to develop that land himself; he wasn't trying to sell it to another real estate man."

"Yeah, right. Lousy idea." Steve tried the foot-swaying trick again. "But who else knew? You, me, Bill Oakes, and . . ."

"And the late Clark Fidey."

"The late Clark Fidey. Yeah."

I opened the door of my antique oaken icebox, refitted with refrigerator coils. "Clark hinted that someone else would be interested in the details of my title search. Then that person offered him so much money that he decided to sell him the bottom-line conclusion and let me wait."

"I get it." Steve pointed to a Sprite and I tossed it to him. "That someone was Gross."

"Mrs. Fidey was vague about the man who visited her son before he died, but she said he was charming and polite, as Herman would have been. He's been charming dithery old women out of their family homes for twenty years." I took a diet cola for myself. Steve doesn't care about calories and I do.

The phone rang. Steve picked it up. Then he nodded at the receiver and handed it to me.

"Frank."

I opened my cola. "Hello, Frank."

"Matt? We just got a preliminary report from the coroner."

"He works fast."

"The post mortem showed we were right about the food poisoning."

"Food poisoning?" I put the phone on the desk speaker so Steve could hear.

"Analysis of the stomach contents shows that he ingested a highly toxic species of inedible mushrooms. Do you want the Latin name?"

"No."

"*Amanita verna*." Frank was reading aloud from a report and there was no stopping him. "They have a heat-stable protein toxin that causes massive cellular damage throughout the body. The liver, kidneys, and central nervous system are destroyed, and the victim becomes disoriented and lapses into a terminal coma."

"How dreadful for him."

"So? What do you think?"

I shrugged at Steve. "I'm speechless."

"I'll have to ask for some loquacity, Matt. We have word that you were with Fidey yesterday when he went shopping at the French Market."

"Half shopping, half mooching, as was his wont."

"I understand that. So where did he get the toadstools that he no doubt thought were mushrooms?"

"Nowhere. Not while I was with him."

Frank has an excellent B.S. detector, even over the phone. But I am an excellent liar when the occasion demands.

I had seen Clark buy mushrooms from Ben. Unquestionable mushrooms. So why get poor Ben in trouble by letting the police do a Tylenol job on him.

I hurtled along. "He was bragging that he'd scored

some great mushrooms for his dinner. But he never opened his shopping bag to show me."

"Is that how it went, Matt?"

"He might have picked them in Washington Square, for all I know."

Supercop issued a dangerous silence, then gave it up. "Oh nuts, why should you lie? No one thinks you did it."

"You're welcome. Any time."

When I hung up the receiver, Steve was nodding and bouncing.

"So Herman Gross killed Fidey?"

"Herman Gross couldn't kill a bottle of seltzer." I added ice to my pop and resumed my seat.

"Then who fed Fidey those toadstools?"

"Who had access to his food supply?"

"No one. He took his last meal at home."

"So?"

"You don't mean . . . ?" Came the dawn and an open mouth. "It couldn't have been Clark's own mother?"

"It couldn't have been anyone else. When I first saw Mrs. Fidey, she was cutting down toadstools in the front yard. She simply scooped up a few and dropped them into his bag of mooched salad ingredients."

"But why would she have done it? There was no motive."

"There was an excellent motive. She wanted his room."

"His room?"

"If you had seen her ruin of a house, you would have understood. That poor woman envisioned living out the remainder of her years among tarps and sawhorses in a crumbling construction site. She must have overheard Clark tell me he was leaving it just that way as long as his mother lived. She knew there was no hope."

"So she substituted toadstools for the mushrooms he'd bought from Ben."

"And hoped for the best. Yes."

"Aren't you going to report her to the police?"

"What for? Mrs. Fidey was drifting on the edge of reality already. And I think this incident has pushed her all the way over. She's shut up in her room now, living in the world of fifty years ago, when her home was the showcase of Marigny and she was the prettiest debutante at the Comus Ball."

Chapter 15
Saturday Evening, March 11th

At three o'clock, Edwina breezed into my office without waiting to be announced. I saw Steve behind her just shrugging and waved him back to his work. I was rising to greet her when she peremptorily pushed me back in my chair.

"I know I'm early. But I couldn't wait to see you."

"Likewise."

"Besides, it's a turn-on to see my man in his work setting. You know, doing these cute little career things."

"Filling out employee tax forms is not cute. For the past hour, I've seen nothing but columns of figures and percentages."

"Maybe you need a change of scenery. I'm all packed for the country."

I reached for her hand. "Me, too."

"Do you love me?"

A casually flung question, but what a wretchedly unfair one under the circumstances. At best there are only two reasonable answers to it. The first is: "Love? What is love, anyway?"

I had an overwhelming sense of kinship with Edwina, took delight in her company, looked forward to seeing her every day, and missed her when she was gone. I felt protective as hell toward the woman. Did all this add up to love?

Also, I wanted her physically, more than I had ever wanted any female. How did lust factor into the equation?

I resorted to the second reasonable answer.

"I've always loved you, Edwina."

"Sort of like a big brother, you mean?"

"Right now, a little more than that."

"Not good enough. I want *much* more."

I stood up, took her face in my hands, and kissed her eyes, one at a time. "I'll be whatever you want me to be, dear."

She pretended to accept that, and I grabbed my coat as I stepped into the showroom, calling to Steve, "I'm leaving early today."

He looked up from an invoice and winked. "Yeah, so would I."

By the time we finally got on the road it was nearly four o'clock. Edwina is so small that she had to adjust the driver's seat on my SEL 500 three times before we got to I-10.

Then we did fifty minutes of small talk about the New Orleans ballet and opera companies while she waited to ambush me with her proposition. She sprang it just south of Donaldsonville.

"Guess what? I saw my gynecologist today."

Suspecting no guile, I considered this as good a drive topic as any.

"Do tell me all about it."

"It was scary in a way. Old Doctor Stein sort of slyly noted that I was pre-gravida and asked my age. When I said thirty-five last birthday, he said there's nothing wrong with me, understand. But if I ever want any children, I'd better get on the ball."

"I see."

"Then you understand that it's time we got married."

Luckily I was wearing my harness or I would have slipped right out of my seat. "Beg pardon? 'We'?"

"My biological clock is running down. Don't you read the magazines? It's a very trendy thing that millions of women of our generation have chosen careers over motherhood. And now, as they reach the end of their childbearing years, they stop to reconsider the path they've taken. They start daydreaming about Lamaze, two o'clock feedings, diaper services, back-to-school sales, teacher conferences—"

I broke in before she got to First Holy Communion. "Yes, I understand all that. But, darling, what has it to do with me?"

"You're nearly thirty-eight yourself, Matty."

"Entirely thirty-eight."

"Don't you like children?"

"I'm not sure. I don't know any."

"Well, you couldn't have given up the idea of having them."

"Not altogether."

I've often considered the possibility of fatherhood. Every man feels some obligation to perpetuate his name. Also, I'd like to have somebody to leave my money to.

"Then what could be more natural than you and me? We like the same people, the same parties. And we're both 'winters,' so our clothes will always be color coordinated."

"That's true compatibility, all right."

"Think what a team we'd make. Together we could breed some beautiful little Devon-Sinclairs and send them to Le Monde des Infants for Montessori training."

"The clothes and the kids are all well and good. But what about the life I have now?"

"That gay stuff?" She waved it off. "You wouldn't have to make much of an adjustment. Almost every husband cheats on his wife with *somebody*. So just do your sneaking around with Robin. Or the boy of the week. I don't care, so long as you don't get a disease."

"That reminds me of my friend Rod York."

"I don't know him."

"He was inveigled into marriage by this Italian girl from Gentilly. She swore up and down that his gay life-style wouldn't bother her."

"And did it?"

"No. Because the minute the vows were said, she completely forgot Rod was homosexual. And then the new Mrs. York wouldn't let him out alone after six in the evening."

"How unfair!"

"No kidding. I ran into the wretch just a year later and he had aged ten with frustration. He'd lost weight. His eyes had dark rings around them . . ."

"The poor man!"

"The moral of the story is: When a normally sexed woman marries a fruit, *one* of them is going to be miserable."

"But that awful woman was Italian, you said. They're known to be unreasonable, right?" She reached over and squeezed my arm. "We're civilized, after all."

"Some of us are. And I can't help thinking about my rival. Bill Oakes?"

"Thinking what?"

"That the man is hopelessly in love with you."

"Yes. It's cute."

"In a way that I could never love a woman."

"You're not perfect. So?"

"Bill is also athletic, rich, and has no genetic defects. Why not found your dynasty on his seed?"

"Heaven knows I would if he were an orphan. But you don't just marry a man, you know. You marry his whole background." She turned off onto Exit 182. "You should see his family in Mississippi. All Baptists. They eat *possum*, for God's sake!"

"A good woman can civilize a man."

"But not a mother-in-law. I'm not naîve, Matty. I know how you are. And that you could never be everything to me. But still I'd rather have some small part of you than one hundred percent of any other man. We're so much *fun* together. Is that so difficult to understand? —Here's the bridge.—You and I were made for each other. It was fated since we were kids."

"I'm flattered, darling."

I cogitated on that flattery while we crossed the famous Sunshine Bridge of Donaldsonville. At the time of its construction back in '62, this was our country-singing governor's most notorious boondoggle. Jimmie Davis had commissioned the 30 million dollar bridge, a modern twin-span four-lane structure, not minding the fact that it didn't lead anywhere a body wanted to go. The bridge connected two shell roads through swamp lands. It was named after Davis's most famous oeuvre, "You Are My Sunshine."

Governor Davis gave concerts instead of political speeches and won two terms in Baton Rouge. (We Louisiana voters will always choose an entertainer over an administrator.) Davis was known for bringing his palomino into the governor's mansion to watch him sign bills and for ending each session of the legislature by calling his band in to render "It Makes No Difference Now."

With all that, Jimmie Davis was probably as good a governor as we've had since the Sieur de Bienville.

At least he sang on-key.

"We'll be stopping on the highway in Belle Rose," I told my driver. "For our oysters."

"I don't remember any seafood stands up there."

"Well, we're not going to buy them."

At my signal, she turned into the shell drive of an old Acadian-style farmhouse. As we parked under the pecan tree there was no need for the formality of a hooted greeting. The gentleman of the house had spotted us from the field and jumped off his tractor to meet us, waving.

"*Eh, Neg'! Ou t'etais fourer?*"

"*J'etais ici et la bas.* Edwina? This is Roy Robicheaux. He was my foreman on Lay Barge twenty-three, but now he's retired to coonass heaven. A life of shrimp trawling, oyster tonging, and muskrat trapping."

"Dear me, really?" Edwina put her hand out and Roy took it, grinning around his dip of Copenhagen.

"*Mais*, she's a purty little t'ing. But she don't speak French?"

"Only *chu de poule*."

"Well, you might can teach her to talk right."

Edwina took my arm. "What does he mean, Matty? Of course I speak French."

"But only the European dialect. Cajuns call that 'chicken ass French' because of all the silly puckering."

Roy and most other lower parish Cajuns trace their ancestry back to the Acadians who were exiled from Canada in 1755. My Fontenot relatives midstate are not Cajuns in the strictest sense, being descended from French settlers who never saw Canada. But all Louisiana French are called Cajuns these days, and we have no trouble understanding one another.

"Hey, Matt." Roy offered, "I sure am glad to see you wit' a girl this time. I was beginnin' to t'ink dey was somet'in' wrong wit' you."

"There are a million things wrong with me, Roy. Chief among which is that I'd like to eat fresh oysters tonight and don't have any."

"*Mais*, you sure did stop in de right place, Neg'. Look what all I got back underneath the garage."

Keeping cool in the shade of the garage were three hundred-pound gunny sacks of oysters. My mouth watered just seeing the sacks.

"Done made my run and sold at the dock, but I still got the best salty oysters here. And the old lady, she ain't gonna want to clean 'em all, so take you a couple sacks."

"We have a small party, Roy. One sack is all we could possibly consume."

I felt a cold wet muzzle on the back of my hand and reached behind me to pet it. "Hi, Phideaux."

Edwina drew back. "Do you know this dog?"

"*Mais* sure," Roy told her. "Matty knows too much about animals to turn his back on one he ain't acquainted wit'."

"But he's such a strange-looking creature, with that weird piebald marking. And those blue eyes."

"Phideaux here is a purebred Catahoula hound." I informed her. "The only breed originating in Louisiana."

"*Mais*, he can track a rabbit t'rough a river of gumbo. Catahoula's the smartest dog goin'." Roy went down on the ground to wrestle with his pride and came up gritty and wet. "Hey, I been tryin' to give Matty a pup, but he don't want."

"Blanche would get jealous. She's at that time of life."

After I heaved my prize into the car trunk, Edwina took the wheel, checked her lipstick in the rear-view mirror, and turned us back on Highway 308 along Bayou La Fourche.

"Roy is quite a colorful character," she observed after half a mile.

"A fast-disappearing breed."

"And a good man to know when you need oysters. You haven't worked off-shore since law school. How did you stay in touch with him all these years?"

"Roy called me right after I graduated from Loyola. His old *Ma-mere* wanted to make out her will, and there are very few lawyers who can write French."

"Why did she care about that?"

"Because she didn't speak English, and she wanted a will she could understand."

"A reasonable request."

"A will may be executed in any language, so these old Cajuns can be accommodated if someone knows enough and cares enough to do it. I handle all the Robicheauxs' legal work."

"Well, of course you learned French in school. But when did you pick up that Cajun dialect?"

"Back while I was growing up. My parents traveled to Europe every year, so they used to ship me off to my Fontenot cousins in Grand Prairie."

"Ooh!" She made a face in the rear-view mirror. "Why did they send you there?"

"Why not? It was cheaper than camp and at least as healthy. I got to go barefoot all summer, except for Mass."

"A little too rustic for my taste. My idea of 'roughing it' is a night at the old Plantation House—twenty-one rooms on Bayou La Fourche, and it has so much history. Don't you envy Geoff and Ondine?"

"Not a bit. That place is a cancer. The house devours all the money they make and all their spare time."

"I think Geoff can afford it," Edwina said.

Geoff Ramsey was in my class at Loyola Law School. Then after graduation we served together in the D.A.'s office and starved together on $11,000 a year parish pay.

Now Geoff is doing $60,000 as a civil court judge, which is almost as much as I clear selling furniture. And Ondine makes a respectable living producing "Couples Tell." But between them, they still don't make enough to keep the ancestral home fully staffed and in good repair. Fortunately, the place is of sufficient historical interest to attract tours and overnight paying guests. Their admission fees at least support the maid and the grounds keeper.

The two-story Greek Revival mansion was designed by an Irish architect named Henry Howard and built in 1846 for a Louisiana colonel and sugar cane grower. Geoff is the old colonel's great-great grandson descended through the female line.

This was a work weekend. The staff had been given three days off and we were on our own. So I carried our suitcases through the wide entrance hall and headed for the Lee bedroom. It's not called after the great general himself but after the magnificent half-tester bed and matching pieces, manufactured in 1840 by a Cincinnati craftsman named Lee and transported down the Mississippi on a flatboat before the Civil War.

I unpacked and hung our natural fibers in the armoire before joining the others in the kitchen. Unlike most kitchens built at the same time, this one is attached to the main house, separated only by a thick fire wall. It still has the original wood-burning stove, copper cream separator, and smoke bench. But there is also a new gas range with microwave oven under the Clementine Hunter original on the fire wall.

Ondine turned a sinfully luxurious cut of beef in the marinade. "Welcome to a weekend of hard work and waiting on yourself."

"Thank you, dear. I'm delighted."

Ondine Bourge Ramsey is my second cousin, which is no particular distinction. All the old families around here are interrelated in some way. She has a figure that used to be described as "pleasingly plump." There's just a little too much of everything but in the right places.

"Donnie and Gordon are staying at their grandma's tonight. So we'll just be adults here." She laughed, tossing her head. "To use the term loosely."

Her helpmeet, Geoff, had already opened my sack of oysters and was hunkered down on the floor, shucking them as efficiently as any river Cajun.

"With the kids gone, the four of us can pretend it's nineteen sixty-eight again and we're all twenty years old. Anybody want to smoke a joint?"

"Not me," I said. "I eat too much when I toke. And my gut knows perfectly well it's not twenty years old."

Edwina had already rolled up her sleeves and was at the cutting board. "I'm nice enough to chop your vegetables for you." She tried to feed me a mushroom but I ducked away.

"Where did you get that?"

"French Market. Where'd you think?"

"I don't know. Maybe outside."

"He's paranoiac, poor dear. He spent Wednesday afternoon with Jessica Clouet and he knows I'm jealous."

"She's beautiful, elegant, and extremely well guarded." I knew where they kept the double boiler, so I took it down and grabbed the milk, butter, and flour to start my French white sauce.

Edwina attacked a sheaf of green onions. "I remember how angry we all were when Jessica married Cowboy."

"I can understand that."

"Yes. We all said, 'What does he see in her?' Here he was, a famous rodeo star, and she was just a schoolgirl."

"What I see in her is that she's wealthy." Geoff lifted an elbow to get leverage with his oyster knife. "That spread across the lake must be worth close to a million. And half is Jessica's in her own right."

I shook my spices into the pot.

"Are you sure?"

"My father was the Clouets' attorney, so he handled the settlement. It was just paperwork, though. There was no contest."

Ondine wiped her hands, opened the cupboard, and brought out a Tarot deck. "But why does she still live with him? . . . Here, Matty, shuffle the cards.'

"The divorce was only a formality so the Cowboy could take another wife. They never intended to split up."

'Gosh, she's awfully understanding."

"Geoff, save the juice from the oysters. I'm going to use it in the sauce." I opened Ondine's wooden box and untied the silk handkerchief.

Edwina said, "I think a man should have as many women as he can make happy." Then she stretched like a cat who had been made happy.

Tarot cards are bigger and more awkward to handle than the kind you play bridge with. I pivoted some, then shuffled according to instructions. Four times, then seven times, then nine times.

Geoff bootlegged a particularly succulent oyster, diverting it to his mouth. "Same thing happened with Carmen in her turn: divorce, more than generous settlement, and then she just sort of forgot to leave when he married Missy." He opened another and held the half-shell out to Edwina. She accepted the oyster with a curtsy. "He'd better not try for number four though. He flat can't afford it."

"You finished?" Ondine took the cards from me and arranged them on the sideboard. "This is you, king of pentacles, the businessman."

"Why can't I be king of swords?" I queried petulantly.

Geoff said, "Let him be king of cups. The drunk."

"No," Edwina said. "He should be king of wands, the guy with the big stick."

"Thank you."

Ondine ignored all of us. "This one covers you. Six of swords—a very important decision you have to make. This one crosses you. Six of cups—an emotional decision."

"So far you've got it right."

"This is above you." She didn't name the card, but I saw.

"La Mort? That's death!"

"But the death card doesn't mean death," Ondine said quickly. "It's good. It means a change."

"Death brings on a lot of meaningful changes of a lasting nature."

She placed another card. "This is beneath you, at the base of the matter—Le Pendu: the hanged man."

Edwina stood next to me to look down at the card. "The hanged man?" The wall phone jingled and Geoff rose to answer it.

"Yes? Right here, Donnie. . . . Hon? It's the boys calling."

"I'll take it in the living room."

Ondine laid the deck on the sideboard and walked

out, leaving a heavy silence behind her. Edwina finally broke it.

"Well, he isn't hanged like poor Brad. This fellow is hanging upside down by his foot. By the foot isn't so bad, is it?"

"Not so good," Geoff allowed. "But not exactly fatal either. I mean, right side up is much worse."

I used the moment to check on my sauce, which hadn't started bubbling, but there wasn't time to mince the yellow onion before Ondine swept back in. "They needed formal permission to watch 'Miami Vice.' I said, 'Why not?' I love the clothes." She looked around at us, then realized she was the only one talking. "Oh! Back to the cards. Listen, Matty, the hanged man only means a time of introspection, a reevaluation of your personal philosophy."

"Oh? Is that all it means?"

"Yes. That's right . . . This is behind you: the magician. You felt in charge of things before, but now you don't.'

Edwina leaned over the table, chin on hands. "I hope that means *I'm* in charge now."

The seer went on with the reading. "This is ahead of you. The lightning-struck tower."

"I'm sorry I came."

"Well, it does mean a crisis. But it's sort of a cleansing destruction. You may tear down your present way of life and build it up again better. . . . This is you. The fool."

"She's right. Give me my cap and bells."

"This is the people around you—the moon." Ondine pushed her hair back. "Someone around you is deceiving you, Matty. And it's a dangerous deception, too. Because the next card is the seven of swords—danger in the dark."

"That's true for anyone who lives in the city."

"There's one last card, so don't worry. And it's—" She shook her head. "Damn! Knight of swords reversed."

"Just a guy on a horse upside down," Geoff said.

"Could be me. I was on Edwina's horse Wednesday, and my position was precipitously reversed."

Ondine looked around at all of us. "No, this isn't Matty. This is an evil, violent, destructive person"—she pointed to the seven—"who wants to kill him."

Chapter 16
Saturday Night, March 11th

After preparing our own meal like servants in the kitchen, we all retired to our rooms and dressed in semifinery. Geoff and I wore Edwardian-style smoking jackets over ruffled shirts while the ladies climbed into antebellum costumes with decolletage and full skirts of rustling velvet. Then we all dined by candlelight like lords and ladies of the manor, picking our side dishes off the sterling lazy susan.

The first two oysters we ate raw and ungarnished. The next two had been spritzed with lemon juice, and then came three dipped in hot cocktail sauce. The main appetizer was my baked oyster concoction, and all diners were properly appreciative.

Edwina asked, "What do you call this dish, Matty?"

Geoff said, "I call it 'good.' Give Ondine the recipe."

"There's no recipe. Just sauté your vegetables in butter, add a little white wine, grated cheese, bread crumbs—"

"How much of each?"

"Enough."

Ondine pulled over another six "Oysters Good" on the half shell. "Don't bother to ask him for quantities. He never measured anything in his life."

"I improvise all my dishes, so they never come out the same way twice. I learned to cook by watching Tante Prudence. She used to measure all her ingredients *à l'oeil* and somehow it came out right."

Ondine said. "The only English words she knew were 'You wanna eat?' And of course I always did."

179

Edwina looked suspicious. "What do you know about Matty's aunt?"

"I spent one summer with them. That was the year Clementine persuaded my parents to go with them on the *Queen Mary*." She cut an oyster daintily to make it last two bites. "I think it's an old French custom. Parisians used to send their bothersome children off to the provinces to live with the peasants."

I spooned more white sauce onto Edwina's oysters.

"Nonc and Tante would get a hundred dollars to take me for the summer, and it was found money. I didn't cost them a nickel to keep."

"There's always more than enough fresh, natural food on a farm," Ondine said. "And the life was glorious. Every morning I got to throw corn to the chickens and milk Caillette, Tante's spotted cow."

"By the end of that one summer, Ondine was speaking Cajun like a native."

"There was no choice. The old people didn't understand English. But I loved the sheer primitivism of the place. There was nothing to read all summer but the sign in front of Bordelon's General Store: 'Regal Beer Tastes Better Over Here.' "

"Nonc Aldus would hitch up the wagon and drive down to Bordelon's for a fifty-pound block of ice and a sack of rock salt. Meanwhile, Ta-tante would be whipping up Caillette's fresh cream with eggs still warm from the hens."

"And I'd get out the *sabotierre*, the ice cream freezer." I poured Edwina more milk. "We'd put peat sacks on the freezer for insulation, then make Ondine sit on it."

"Froze my *chu*."

"The kids would spell each other at the hand crank until they couldn't move it anymore, then a grown-up would take over. When the ice cream got too thick for anyone to crank, then *'c'est fait.'* "

Ondine put down her fork. "Mind you, that was pure ice cream, made with one hundred percent fresh ingredients. I remember that Matty did most of the cranking. But he let me lick the beaters anyway. Wasn't that sweet of him?"

"That depends," Geoff said, with his mouth full. "What'd you let *him* lick?"

After dinner, I sprang up and began clearing the dishes to advertise that I was not a male supremacist. But Ondine shooed me away.

"Thanks for the thought, Matty. I'm just going to pile these in the dishwasher."

"If you don't need me, I'll have a chance to confer with your old man. Geoff? How about meeting me in the library. I left my papers there."

Edwina thrust out her lip. "Are you two sneaking off for a bull session?"

"We're only going to talk law. But cows are welcome if you want to audit."

"That dry stuff? I'll have more fun helping Ondine load the dishwasher." And off she flounced, swinging her crinolines.

Geoff carried his brandy into the library and sat back on the antique sofa. It was hand-carved of rosewood a hundred and fifty years ago by a German named Belter. The original velvet covering had long since rotted away and been replaced, but otherwise the piece was exactly as first manufactured.

"I love to talk legal theory, if you don't think this is likely to end up in my court."

"I should be so lucky." I opened my briefcase. "These are the papers Clark Fidey dug up for me in the Mint and the Supreme Court Law Library. I spent all morning sorting through the mess, and there's only one way to make it. We don't have clear title to the riverfront property."

"From what I understand, your mother's family has owned that land a hundred years."

"It was deeded to my great-great-great grandfather,

Francis Vigé, after the War Between the States. But the cloud goes back further than that." I read from my notebook. "Follow this if you can: Francis Vigé married one Emelie Mouton in 1860, and she bore him eight children. But only two, John and Pauline, lived to adulthood. Emelie died in 1878, so Francis, after the custom of the time, took a second wife, Agnes Breaux, and started all over. He had one son by her, Henry, and then he died intestate."

Geoff whistled. "You have documents to prove all that?"

"All from the archives. The estate, which was a large one, was divided among the widow and surviving children. The riverfront property passed on to John and Pauline, Emelie's children."

"Is that the legacy under dispute? Could there have been a will? Maybe a holographic one?"

"No chance. Francis could barely write his name."

"Suppose he had children not accounted for."

"Got church records—birth, baptism, and death for each one. All in a row. Pauline died without issue and her portion passed to John. Since then, the property has passed through an unbroken line of Vigés to my mother, the last of John's branch of the family."

Geoff sipped his beer and shrugged. "Sounds airtight to me. Where's the cloud?"

Brad burrowed through the city records like a rodent until he found something rather nasty in the census of eighteen twenty." I held out Bill's photocopy. "Emelie Mouton's mother, Therese Coulet, was a child of two during this census, and it's clear from the record that she was a quadroon."

Geoff chewed thoughtfully. "You're sure Therese was Emelie's mother?"

"I followed it right down the line, matching names and birth dates. Yes, the connection is made and would be upheld in court."

"I see."

"So Emelie herself looked white, but she had to be an octoroon: a Negro under Louisiana Law. You're an attorney, so you have a good idea of the ramifications." I unfolded photocopied pages from the Civil Code and read aloud: "Impediments of direct line relationship: miscegenation."

This entry was written in 1894, so my eye traveled down to a former Code from 1808, page 24. I starred Article 3 and handed it over to Geoff. He read aloud: " 'Free persons and slaves are incapable of contracting marriage together; the celebration of such marriages is forbidden, and the marriage is void; it is the same with respect to the marriages contracted by free white persons with free people of color.' So there it is in—excuse the expression—black and white. 'The marriage may be impeached by the parties themselves, by any persons interested, or by the Attorney General.' "

"And Brad was sure as hell interested," I said. "So are a lot of other people."

He handed the papers back and shook his head. "Those old laws against miscegenation probably wouldn't be upheld all the way to the Supreme Court."

"*If* we were granted certiorari. And I doubt this conservative court would soil its dainty hands on that particular bucket of worms."

"Unfortunately, you're right. *They're* right. So at the very least, Brad could have drowned you in ink and tied you up in litigation for years. Have title insurance?"

"You kidding? We've had that parcel a hundred years." I slapped the paper down. "You know what stinks? If Francis and Emelie had only waited ten more years, it would have been legal. Between 1870 and 1894 that statute wasn't in force. So when Emelie's children contracted marriages, theirs were valid, even though they were legally negroes."

"What about the next generation?"

"Those children were only one-thirty-second Negro,

which made them legally white under the law. Their marriages were recognized, too."

"So we've got only one bad link in the chain."

"And that's all they need. The marriage of Francis to Emelie was null. The children were bastards, and their claim would be entirely superseded by a legitimate heir."

'And Francis had other issue."

"His son Henry, by·the white woman Agnes Breaux. He was Vigé's single legitimate heir. Get the picture?"

"So after more than a hundred years, the descendents of Henry Vigé have a claim on the property."

"That acreage is worth millions. Or it will be if the casino goes through. So all Brad had to do was go through the records of births and marriages and trace down those heirs.

"You think that's what he did?"

"And I think that's what he told me the morning he died."

"Oh? Do you finally remember?"

"There are pieces floating around in my head, and I've been snatching at them trying to assemble one complete thought. But that must have been what I was so angry about." Imagining how to tell my mother that she was losing her most valuable piece of real estate. That was the worst part.

But what I said to Geoff was, "Suppose Brad located the descendents of Henry Vigé and bought out their interest."

"If so, why haven't they come forward?"

"It's possible they never knew what they were selling. There are ways to do that."

'Sure, missing heir schemes," Geoff said. "Joe Shmoe comes up to me and says, 'Hey, stranger, I'll pay you two hundred dollars for your interest in City Park Lake.' So I say, 'Gee, I don't have any interest at all in City Park Lake. I'm getting the two hundred for nothing.' Then it turns out that Shmoe has been through the Office of Deeds and Records and discovered that a hundred and fifty years ago my great grandpappy won City Park Lake in a poker game. So I *did* have a claim on that real estate, which *he* can now sell for a million."

"And wouldn't you be mad?"

"You bet your ass I'd be mad." He grinned. "I might even *kill* Joe Shmoe."

"But there's a rainbow ahead. I think Clark Fidey found it before he . . . um . . . died accidentally."

Geoff looked alert. "He told you that?"

"In his own word, 'indisputably.' Clark called me to say he had good news and bad news about my ancestry."

"Hah! That's an old joke. The bad news is that you're wiped out. The good, that he'll let you jump off his roof."

"He swore it was something I'd want to hear." I hefted the pile of photocopies. "But then he said he wrote his conclusions down on a piece of yellow legal paper, and that one is gone."

"Gone where?"

"Sold to Herman Gross, who slithered in this very morning trying to buy my interest."

"Then Clark's findings were favorable." My good host rose and emptied his brandy snifter. "You've got the answer somewhere in that collection of papers. If he found it, then there's no reason why you can't do the same."

By the time the dinner dishes were washed and dried, it was after ten and all the stars were out. The stars and the moon. Ondine went upstairs to turn down the beds. Edwina took our host's arm and steered him through the ballroom.

"You know I think this house would be a perfect setting for a wedding reception."

"It was for ours," Geoff agreed.

"It's a long drive from the city. But there's enough room so that all my bridesmaids can spend the night. We'll have a big house party." She performed a ballerina's turn under the teardrop crystal chandelier. "And the photographers will love it. Can't you see us on the "Weddings" page of *Town and Country*? 'The Matthew Sinclairs, New Orleans, Louisiana.' "

"Oh. So *Matt* is to be the lucky groom?"

"Who else?"

"One never knows with you. Your cast of characters is interchangeable."

Geoff and Edwina stepped outside to shiver under the crisp night breeze blowing in from the bayou.

Left in a moment of solitary reflection, I brought my drink to the library to enjoy the view of the terrace through the open French windows.

Piaf and Sarapo's "A Quoi Ça Sert l'Amour" was coming from the hidden stereo speakers. I kicked off my shoes and lay back on the Napoleon day couch to enjoy the ballad.

A young man seeking advice about the secrets of love asks:

> What is it for, this love?
> They always tell stories that make no sense.
> What good is it to love?

And the wanton and dissolute older woman replies:

> Love doesn't explain itself.
> It comes we know not from where.
> And it takes us all in a blow.

It's better in French.

While listening to Piaf and Sarapo deal with the universal subject, I idly observed Edwina and Geoff playing "Me boy; you girl" out on the terrace, framed by pins of starlight against the velvet sky.

She did a Loretta Young twirl in her crinolines and waved her fur boa under his chin. He bent over into kissing range and told her something I didn't hear. Then they laughed together.

As the drink cooled and warmed me, I picked up the

album cover for *Piaf and Sarapo at the Bobino*. Here was a photograph of the diminutive "French sparrow" at forty-seven, a shriveled toad of a woman but still an irresistable presence for her lusty hedonism. Beside her stood twenty-four-year-old Theo Sarapo, the handsome and adoring husband. The cover portrait had been taken early in 1962, less than a year before the great conflagration that was Piaf finally consumed itself—died of too much living. And five years after that, the handsome young Sarapo was to follow her by way of an auto crash. But here on this album cover at least, they remain forever alive and warm and in love.

Sarapo sang the eternal question:

> Me, I've heard it said that love makes one suffer.
> That love makes one cry.
> What good is it to love?

And Piaf the only honest answer:

> Love is good for this,
> To give you joy with tears in your eyes.
> It's sad and marvelous.

Ondine swept through the library with swaying skirt, carrying her drink. "So here's where you'd got to. I was looking for you." She picked up my feet just to slip beneath them and held them comfortably on her lap as she sipped.

"Lonely, Matty?"

"No."

"Happy?"

"Not that either. Say, cousin, how do you think I'd look with a beard?"

"Like a Camp Street derelict. Why?"

"Because I may just give up shaving. Every morning now, I have to look in the bathroom mirror and count more gray hairs. And then the reflection dims and changes and I can see myself twenty and thirty years from now growing old alone. There I am, a dessicated old auntie crouching on my front stoop just praying that some chicken will stop and talk to me."

"You're getting maudlin. All the old queens I know are happier than old single men who are straight."

"But if I were straight, I wouldn't be single. I wouldn't be shacked up with a female equivalent of Robin either."

"Who knows if you were straight? Maybe you would be going bald. Maybe you wouldn't have your sense of style and color. Maybe you wouldn't be as charming."

"Maybe I'd be dull as dust. All the better to settle into a semblance of normal domestic life."

She patted my toes. "Speaking of normal, you've never brought a woman up here before. Is it serious between you and Edwina?"

"Getting grimmer by the day. Why?"

"She told me she's proposed to you."

"Isn't that strange? What could she have been thinking of?"

"That fact that you're a very desirable man, albeit bisexual."

"But I'm not bisexual, dear. That implies fifty-fifty. With me it's more like eighty-twenty."

She started a game of "piggy went to market" through my argyles. "In this world of halfways and near misses, maybe that's close enough."

"Ondine, you know I like women and always have. Sometimes I even fall in love with one of them. But it's only for a little while. Ever since I was aware of having any sexuality at all—I think I was six—I've been attracted to the male form. So my grand passions have always been for men. I mean, if ever you catch me with my head in the oven, *cherchez l'homme!* "

"In your case it's usually *cherchez le* football player!.' But refer back to your Tarot cards. That lightning-struck tower means you can change your entire way of life."

"I don't really have the will to— That tickles.—My way is natural to me."

"I understand the naturally unnatural well enough." She stopped on my little toe. "And you know that some perfectly nice gay people get married."

"There's no lack of examples, cousin. And I've never had it far from my mind that someday I may setttle into a fantasy of 'Father Knows Best.' There will be a lovely wife I can relate to, kids around the dinner table, and Mass on Sundays."

"Is that what you really want?"

"I can't be sure. But for the past five years, my nightly prayer has gone, 'Oh God, make me straight, but not now.' "

She pinched the "piggy who had roast beef."

"I think Edwina would be your perfect match. You have so much in common, speak the same language, look good together. Why don't you accept her proposal, have lots of little Devon-Sinclairs, and live the American Dream?"

"Give up sex?"

"Oh, but you wouldn't have to do that. I still see . . . friends." She shrugged under her velvet stole.

"Very discreetly."

"Sure, I'd rather make my life with a woman. But if I had, I wouldn't have my two boys. And they mean the world to me. I've made a choice."

"With no regrets?"

"None. If you make just a few adjustments, you'll see that you can be happy leading a normal life."

There was a giggling commotion at the French windows now; Edwina pranced in to join us, leading Geoff by the hand.

"Matty! We thought of a great idea to raise money for the committee!"

"Should I ask? Do I dare?"

"You and I go on 'Couples Tell.' "

"That's a *terrible* idea."

"No, it's not!" Ondine took up their cause, springing from the couch and almost rolling me off onto the floor in her enthusiasm. "Oh, *do* it! An appearance on the show would bring in money for the committee and give you free publicity at the same time. Most of our friends have already been on to raise funds for some cause or another. Besides, you're both so photogenic together—you would make a beautiful couple!"

"That show is premised on humiliation, cousin. You bring on perfectly respectable people and barrage them with embarrassing questions."

"There are no embarrassing questions," she reproached. "Only embarrassing answers. Ask Nixon."

"Oh really? How about What position do you like to make whoopee in?' "

"We never asked that, Matty." Then she vacillated. "Well, maybe you heard 'When do you like to make whoopee?' But it's usually just harmless stuff like . . . oh . . . 'Do you know Edwina's favorite movie?' "

"*The Man Who Fell to Earth!*" Edwina prompted. "Or anything with David Bowie. Oh, he's so exciting, Matty. I dated him once."

"Big deal. So did I. My favorite movie is *Spartacus*."

"With Tony Curtis? Yeesh."

"See? That's not so personal." Ondine cajoled. "Or they might ask Edwina, 'What's Matt's favorite dish?' "

"Snapping Turtle Sauce Piquante." I admitted.

Ondine held both my hands. "See? It's very painless really. Just good clean fun. Plus you'd be getting me out of a spot for this week's taping. We've lined up our couples from the sports and entertainment worlds, but we're still missing one."

"One ordinary couple?"

"Well, you can put it that way. Tootie and Geraldine Jones are coming, and so are Octave Doucet and his wife."

They were breaking me down. "I've known Octave all my life. And Tootie and Geraldine are good people."

"See? It will be fun!" Edwina bounced up and kissed me. It was all settled.

Chapter 17
Sunday Night, March 12th

I was both keyed up and exhausted by the time our weekend in the country was officially over and Edwina had dropped me off at my front gate. I locked it behind me, then crossed the porch and let myself in the front door. Robin was already waiting in the foyer and rushed to take my coat almost reverently. I noticed that the house had been tidied far beyond Sigrid's capabilities.

"Matty? Tell me just . . ." He stammered and tried again. "How was your excursion with your peer group?"

"Very eventful." I shucked my clothes as I went through to the bedroom and, as per his habit, he trailed along behind picking them up. "Edwina asked me to marry her."

"Marry her!" he screeched. "You can't! You're gay!"

"Oh, you noticed that, too?" I unbuttoned my shirt and handed it over to save him the trouble of stooping. "But I'm also approaching middle age. And consider that I may want to have children before I get too old to play piggy-back."

"You don't want children. You just want little Sinclairs!"

"Why not? As the last male member of my line, I have reason enough to seek legitimate heirs."

"But not with Edwina." His voice got whiney. "The woman isn't exactly a virgin."

"Neither am I."

"But what makes you so sure she would remain faithful to you?"

"My dear, who on earth would want her to?"

Robin dropped my Bruno Magli shoe. "What?"

"When a woman is having an affair, she becomes radiant and exciting. She gives marvelous parties and begs to be mounted a dozen times a day." I unbuttoned my trousers and let them fall. "I much prefer the ravishing adultress to some gray frump who has lost all interest."

"That's very liberal of you. You can't keep it up for a woman, so you'll let someone else do the dirty work."

"Scoff all you like." The bed was already turned down. I sat there to pull my socks off. "But I had a most enlightening chat with a certain lesbian who has found fulfillment with a husband and children."

"Your cousin Ondine?"

"She advised me to go ahead and get married. Her message was that gay people can be quite happy in a straight relationship. With just a few adjustments."

"Adjustments?" He sorted: shirt to laundry, suit to cleaners, tie back to closet. "Like throwing out one bothersome little queen?"

"I wouldn't have to throw you out. You could stay here as long as you like." I slipped under the covers. It wasn't cold enough tonight to force me into pajamas, and I like the feel of satin against my skin.

"Oh yeah? And where would *you* stay?"

"With Edwina, of course. If we were married, I'd have to."

"Then you would just keep me here a shameful secret like Susan Hayward in *Back Street*?" Robin turned away and crumbled my undershirt. "I can see myself growing old and ravaged with the years; sneaking around to meet you maybe once a month for a stolen kiss."

"I hardly think—"

"No life. No future." There was a break in his voice. "Despised by my betters."

"Don't overdramatize. You're only nineteen, for pity's sake. You can go anywhere and be anything you want."

"But I want to stay here and be yours. I haven't even looked at another man since the day we met." He looked back at me and I saw that his face was wet. "Don't you love me?"

"Love? What is—? Sure I do. Of course."

He wiped his eyes with the undershirt. "I know what we've got is just supposed to be temporary—you're sowing your oats or something. But right now you're my whole life, Matty."

I believed that he meant it, or thought he did. I held my arms out. "Come on, kitten. Nothing has been decided yet."

He lifted the cover and crawled into bed beside me, nestling against my chest. "If I could have babies for you, I would. But what can I do about that?"

There was no answer, of course. So I just held him.

Chapter 18
Monday Morning, March 13th

I rose with the sun, wrapped up in the oldest wool robe still in constant use, and lit the gas heater in my study.

Clark's pile of photocopies had to be sorted, read through, and resorted until they yielded up their one- and two-hundred-year-old secrets. Fidey had been the best historical researcher in the city. And now I was left to resort to the distant second best. Me, *moi-meme*.

Just before seven, Robin pulled himself out of bed, my bed, and turned on "Breakfast Edition" before starting our coffee.

"We'll be able to have lunch together, won't we?" His tone wasn't hopeful. For good reason.

"Not today. I've got to work like a beaver at the shop till three, then I promised to run over to Ondine's TV station. We're taping 'Couples Tell' this afternoon."

He brightened. "You and me?"

"Don't be an idiot. New Orleans is pretty decadent, but it's not yet ready for a gay couple on a family show. . . . Where's my coffee? . . . Edwina will be my partner."

"Then your partner Edwina should be getting your coffee right now. That's what she should be doing." He stopped at the TV to change the channel before checking the percolator.

"You'd better wear your camelhair coat. Bob Breck predicts it'll be in the fifties all day."

"Bob Breck can't be more than five feet tall. What would he know?"

"He graduated from the University of Michigan. They say that right there on television."

Robin finally managed to bring me my mug of coffee, hot enough to warm the whole room, and picked up a barely readable photocopy to make room for it on the desk.

"What's this? All I can read is the date, seventeen-fifteen."

"Because it's in French." I took it from him. "A simple chattel transfer. This must have been a slave my ancestor, Louis Vigé, bought to work in his house. . . . No, it's too early. . . . Holy mackeral!"

I had seen this bill of sale during countless shufflings through the pile but hadn't realized its significance before. Fidey had.

"This is going to be *it*, Robin! The title is ours."

He put his hand on my shoulder and shook his head. "What does it mean?"

"It's the good news and bad news about my ancestry, just as Fidey said."

Chapter 19
Monday Afternoon, March 13th

I was exactly on time, at three thirty, and Edwina met me at her door, knotting a thin silk scarf at her throat.

"We can't make love, Matty. It's my time of the month."

"What does that have to do with it?"

"It's just that I have no energy these days."

My protest was only token gallantry. Actually I would have had enormous difficulty accommodating her at the moment. Robin had pumped me dry that morning, resorting even to the hot water trick in a very transparent sabotage of my courtship.

"I hope it wasn't a mistake to wear white." And she twirled around to show off her soft wool ensemble of peplum jacket over a slim skirt in midcalf length, both in winter white and accentuated by an ice blue blouse. My own clothes complemented hers for style and period, referring to the fifties era of comfortable roominess. I like double-pleated pants because they allow one to breathe without looking baggy.

She strapped on a Cartier tank watch. "It's almost time. Let's take your car." She double-locked her front door, set the burglar alarm, and secured the padlock on her gate. "I was missing you this morning. Why didn't you call?"

I had left Edwina only the night before and was due to meet her within a few hours, but to a female, this was apparently a perfectly logical question. How could

I (callously and insensitively) have gone all morning without assuring her of my devotion?

"I was up to my ears in antique documents, gathering proof that we Sinclairs own a certain parcel of riverfront land, uncontestably. I finally found the vital loophole."

"That's nice. But wasn't there a phone around?"

When we reached the station, Paretti, the floor director, waved us into the TV studio, calling behind him.

"Hey, Ondine?! Your society couple is here!"

I stopped for a confrontation. "Why do you call us that?"

He looked blank and scratched his freckled bald spot. "Well, just look at the two a ya."

Edwina leaned on my shoulder. "Matty, we *do* look sort of John Held-ish."

I let her steer me away, stepping over cables. "For crying out loud, the label 'society' calls up images of Noel Coward–type lounge lizards, hanging around cafes, drinking too much, jumping naked into fountains, and planning silly parties."

"So?"

"So I work sixty hours in the average week." We ducked under a boom mike. "I wouldn't have time to be 'society' if I wanted to."

"No one means any harm. They have to call us something. . . . There's Ondine."

Ondine joined us at a dead run, holding a clipboard in one hand, a stop watch in the other.

"Oh, I'm so glad you two are on time. The other couples are already here. Go to makeup."

"Makeup?"

Octave Doucet was already seated at the makeup table with a napkin in his collar. He waved me over.

"Hey, Matty, *viens-'oir*; I got a story for you."

I've been hearing Octave's stories since we fished the bayous together during my summers in Evangeline Parish. They're always entertaining and never true.

"Oui, j'apres t'ecouter."

"You remember our good friend Mr. Elbe?"

"The accordion player?"

"Yeah, bro'. See, he was up there in Schnook's last Saturday night, squeezin' away at his accordion, playin' the 'Bayou Teche Two-Step,' dancin' around, drinkin' his beer an' havin' a good ol' time, so he didn't know nuttin'."

"Elbe never does."

"Mais yeah. He didn't even know his pants come unsewn in the back and you could see everyt'ing he had dar. So right after he played the Two-Step,' he sat hisself down and dis ol' lady, she come up to him and she say real discreet, *'Tu connais ton sac pend?'*

("Do you know your sack is hanging?")

"So Elbe, he jus' smile real happy and take another drink o' his Dixie an' he say, *'Madame, si tu peux la siffler, mon, je peux la jouer!'* "

("Lady, if you can whistle it, I can play it!")

I was laughing along with him when Edwina joined us at the makeup table.

"What did that man tell you?"

"It's only funny in Cajun."

She assessed her reflection in the lighted mirror. "Do I have enough color in my face?"

"Any more and you'd look like a psychedelic vision." Some technician kept trying to assail me with a powder puff. I swatted him away. "This isn't the stage you know. The cameras come up close."

"Ooh, I look ghastly." She made a face but accepted the man's powder puff. "I should have had my hair done."

The stagehands finished lugging the set together and we were bidden to make ourselves stiffly uncomfortable on one of the three Georgian settees. It had been Ondine's idea to eschew the network game show look for her program and instead try to lend "Couples Tell" the look of a genteel after-dinner parlor game. The fake wall backdrop was papered in a subdued lilac pattern. We contestants got to crowd into Louis Quatorze–style love seats and scribble evasive answers to rude questions on vermillion tablets with fake quill pens. Vases of fake flowers decorated the cabriole tables in front of us, which also held real china tea cups.

The master of ceremonies, Bud Hinkler, was to embarrass us from an antique table, where he'd unfold his question cards and read their outrageous contents with the solemnity appropriate to an announcement of the Nobel Prize.

Hinkler had a degree in Communications from Tulane, which qualified him to sell haberdashery on Canal Street forty hours a week. His blond good looks and the fact that he was allowed to borrow suits from his employer won him an on-camera job for one half-hour on Mondays.

As usual, there was no studio audience, so Hinkler didn't have to warm anyone up. Instead he announced the show and players to an imaginary house of wildly applauding fans impersonated just offstage by a sound effects machine.

"From the world of entertainment, we are privileged to welcome jazz great Andrew "Tootie" Jones and his lovely wife, Geraldine."

"Lovely wife, Geraldine" has three chins—or four, depending on the angle of view. But she supported Tootie and their three kids for the first twenty years of the "jazz great's" career, and he was decent enough, or smart enough, not to unload her after he made it.

"And from the sports world, we bring you the winningest jockey ever to grace our Fairgrounds, Octave Doucet and his beautiful bride, Everlina!"

Octave held his hands together over his head to acknowledge the applause; Everlina covered her face and blushed.

Octave makes an easy $100,000 in purses per annum

and could have married any sort of woman he liked—even an "American." But he wanted a bride who spoke French, enjoyed "chank-y-chank" music, and cooked a terrific Ponce Bourée. So, like any good coonass, he had gone back home to Cajun country to find a soulmate. And in fact he had chosen his brother's wife's younger sister, a girl of sixteen. Marrying in-laws used to be a necessity in their isolated culture, where there were no singles' clubs and a man didn't know many people who weren't related to him by blood or marriage; and the practice is still very common among the Louisiana French.

Everlina was a head taller than her husband and quite buxom, which leads one to speculate on the logistics of the mating act. Evidently Octave had got himself a milking stool or whatever was necessary, though, because his bride was visibly pregnant.

"And now we'll meet our society couple, World Cup Competitor Edwina Devon and her fiancé, Matt Sinclair, the antique man— No, just kidding folks. He isn't that old. Matt's fine shop, New Traditions, is one of our sponsors."

Again "society couple"? I wanted to crawl into the crack under the back of the chair. But instead I waved discreetly at the camera. When it was pointed at another fool, I nudged Edwina and whispered, "Fiancé?"

"Well, they needed some kind of identifier. It was either fiancé or 'guy.' They would have introduced you as my 'guy.' Would you like that."

"No."

Hinkler declaimed from the very depths of his diaphragm. "As you know, each correct answer wins a hundred dollars for your team. And the couple with the most correct answers gets a bonus of one—uh—thousand—uh—dollars!"

The sound tech played a tape of a fanfare and another of applause. We contestants acted thrilled at the very notion, Edwina gamely jumping up and down as though dressed as a vegetable on "Let's Make a Deal."

"First we want to state that Tootie and Geraldine Jones will donate all their winnings to the Sickle Cell Anemia Foundation!" (Taped applause.) "Octave and Everlina Doucet are playing for their favorite charity, the S.P.C.A.!" (More taped applause) "And Edwina Devon and Matt Sinclair will be playing for"—he squinted at his card—"the Committee to ... Stop Casino Gambling? In New Orleans?" (Taped applause barely discernible. I strongly suspect that the sound tech suported casino gambling.)

After making the only small talk he was capable of, complimenting the women on their dresses, Hinkler sent them back to the allegedly "soundproofed room," which was really only the ladies' lounge upstairs.

"Here's the first question for you fellas." He tapped a piece of pasteboard. "Tell us, what is your lady's favorite motion picture?"

I caught Ondine winking at me from behind the cameraman and wondered if the fix was in. Tootie said Geraldine liked *The Color Purple*, and Octave was sure Everlina had seen *Rocky IV* three times.

Or was it *Rocky III* four times?

I mentioned Edwina's favorite David Bowie film without going into the facts of her own history with Bowie. And I hoped with all my might that she wouldn't either.

The next question was a zinger.

"Gents? When your lady is feeling 'romantic,' how does she let you know?"

Oh my heavenly days. When Edwina was feeling 'romantic,' as that twit called it, she heaped flowers all over the room, splashed perfume on the light bulbs, "changed into something comfortable ..." It all seemed so pathetically contrived. So when he asked me first, I looked earnest and said, "She gives me a kiss."

"A kiss? That's very nice. And for you, Tootie?"

Tootie replied with implacable dignity, "Geraldine

cooks my favorite meal: roast pork, cornbread, and turnip greens." He smiled. "And then she puts on an Irma Thomas record. That's very romantic."

"It certainly is," Hinkler's empty head bobbed. "Now we go to Mr. Doucet. Octave? What does Everlina do to let you know she's in a romantic mood?"

"*Mais*, she just *show* it to me, bro.' "

"She . . . uh?"

"Yeah, she jus' show me dot t'ing. I get de story all right. Ain't turned it down yet, needer."

"Um . . . Can we put that on?"

By the end of the televised humiliation, Tootie and Geraldine had won the bonus and donated $1800 to Sickle Cell Anemia. (They'd been married thirty years and so had an unfair advantage, I felt.) Octave and Everlina got $600 for their dogs and cats. And our team came up with a miserable $400 for the committee.

I was back at the makeup table scrubbing powder off my face when Mel, the station's anchorman, walked through the studio in his shirt-sleeves holding up a sheet of copy.

"Here's some great news, everyone!" He waved the sheet. "And we can all thank God for those north Louisiana red-ass Baptists. After a debate that lasted all weekend, the legislature just defeated the casino bill!"

Everyone whooped!

Tootie was happy that tourists wouldn't be distracted from his good jazz to pass their evenings chucking dice at the casino.

Octave was gleeful that high stakers would have to continue doing their legal gambling at the track.

And Edwina and I were delirious.

"We're safe again till next year!" She sang out. "The city is safe."

Reverend Jack Dundy had just hurled himself into the studio attired in his telegenic blue shirt and red tie, ready to be interviewed and take all the credit. Edwina and I stayed to listen to his spot.

"The voters of Louisiana want their legislators to do the right thing," he assured Mel. "They're good Christians."

Mel, who isn't Christian, smiled anyway. "So you would say that it was largely religious considerations that defeated the gambling bill?"

"Mostly prayer," the man of God declared with raised hands and trembling voice. "Prayer is what saved this city of ours from sin and corruption."

When he came off the set, I was feeling puckish enough to waylay him, making it look casual.

"Say, Reverend Jack. Did you make your appointment?"

The fat pockets under his eyes crinkled. "What's that?"

"The night we had dinner, remember? You had to meet someone at the Vieux Carre. At *precisely* eight twenty-three."

His big face split into a broad grin.

"Oh yes, suh. That went *very* well. Very well indeed."

The French have a saying: "For every shoe, there's a foot."

Chapter 20
Monday Evening, March 13th

After Ondine gushed a lie that we had just taped the best show ever, Edwina and I took our leave and walked out of the studio together. It was five thirty and just getting dark.

"Matty?" She took my arm proprietarily. "It's a beautiful evening. Let's walk over to K-Paul's for dinner."

"Fair enough, dear. But first I have to check my answering machine."

"Don't you trust Robin to take your messages?"

"Would you?"

No reply. I pulled out my beeper at the first pay phone, dialed my office, and sounded the tone. Four messages came back. George D. returned from Atlantic City, and now (that the question was moot) our committee had his full support. Pierre said he'd enjoyed our chat at the party and asked if I'd mind if he dated Robin. (I would.) Dan, the defrocked priest, called to ask if I'd like to attend a "come as your favorite screen goddess" party at his condo. (I would not.) The last message was the only one that captured my interest. After a click, Charles Eisenhardt's voice came on.

"Matt? This is Cowboy here. I seriously think somebody is trying to *kill* your butt. Call me soon's you can."

"Edwina? Do you have Cowboy's phone number?" She had memorized it on behalf of her horses, so I dialed in four seconds.

Cowboy himself answered on the first ring.

"Yup?"

"This is Matt. I just got your message."

"Glad you called. I was startin' to worry."

"Only starting? I'm an old hand at it."

"Listen, I just checked out that saddle that throw'd you. The cinch was cut-clean through."

"Are you sure?"

"As shootin'. So I had to think on who knew you was comin' and who coulda sawed through the thing."

"In your humble opinion, who?"

"It's just an opinion now. And before I give it, I want to show you this evidence I got up here. You willin' to check it out?"

"I'll be right over."

I had the prescribed dose of phenobarbital back in my system but couldn't yet chance driving, so again Edwina took the wheel. She was too tense and too fast, making a third lane on Claiborne and then cutting in front of a Hubig's truck. I grabbed my armrest and tried to divert her attention.

"Do you want to know about my research?"

She was speeding up the I-10 ramp. "What research?"

"How I'm going to save my mother's parcel of land from the feasting wolves."

"Oh yes. Your loophole." At least she was distracted enough to yield to oncoming traffic on the interstate. "Wasn't your ancestor Emelie Vigé an octoroon after all?"

"She was. And recorded in the eighteen–hundred census as a free woman of color."

Edwina hung a right under the Baton Rouge sign. "So you were blocked."

"Blocked in one direction. But Clark Fidey went backward on the other side. He discovered a bill of sale for Francis Vigé's great-great grandmother. She had been an African woman from the slave coast, sold as a breeder right here in New Orleans."

"That makes Vigé . . . um . . ."

"At least one-sixteenth Negro. According to Louisiana law, that made him black as a Mau Mau chief."

"Then his marriage to Emelie wasn't miscegenation after all."

"No, since they were both black their union was legal, which makes our title clear all the way back. But his subsequent marriage to the white woman Agnes Breaux was null and void. Her heirs have no claim."

"So they were very rich and then very broke in the last three days. It's a mercy on them that they never found out how close they came."

"Maybe they did."

"Why do you think?"

"Rutledge was said to be 'flapping a piece of paper' in my face that morning. I surmise that it was his option on their interest, signed by Henry Vigé's heir or heirs."

"Very possible."

"But no such paper was ever found on him."

She took a moment to digest that. "You think those unknown heirs realized all of a sudden what they had given away? Then they met Brad in his house and took the document from him?"

"I surmise. Though not without killing him first."

"But we don't even know who they are?"

"We will when we go through the records at the Mint. Or when they come forward to press their claim. Whichever comes first."

"Then the question is solved. The riverfront parcel is yours. And not only that, but you can contest title to all the property that went to Henry Vigé. I bet your mother will be thrilled."

"She'll never know."

"Aren't you going to press the claim? It could mean millions."

"It couldn't be worth years of time and court costs. Not to mention going public about my 'roots'."

"You're right, of course." She took her hand off the

gear shift to hold mine. "But so long as we all hush about it, I won't mind the tiniest smidgen of tarbrush in my children."

"Whose children?"

"Ours, Matty." She tapped my knee proprietarily. "I'm used to getting what I want."

"You will, darling."

When we drove onto the Eisenhardt grounds, Cowboy was already waiting in front of the house, wearing a warm sheepskin coat. It's colder north of the lake than south, and he was better prepared than we to meet the near-freezing night.

But he looked startled to see Edwina.

"Unexpected pleasure, gal. Thought Matt would be comin' by himself."

"I can't drive yet," I told him.

"Well, I'm sorry she had to go to all that trouble."

"I don't mind the trip," Edwina said quickly. "I'll just go inside and visit with Jessica."

"Can't, though. The ladies and the kids done went to the horse show up in Baton Rouge." He consulted his watch. "They'll be back in an hour, though. . . . Got somethin' to show you in the tack room. C'mon."

We followed his broad back around the house to the stables. The horseshoe over the doorway had lost a nail and hung askew.

Eisenhardt's tack room was to our right. The inside wall was covered with ribbons and photos of prize horses taking high fences.

The saddle under suspicion had been laid out on the work table.

Edwina skittered over. "Ooh, this is my best English leather saddle."

"It's only the cinch," Eisenhardt assured her. "I can fix it easy. But I thought Matt ought to see the damage first."

I held the shredded strap up to the swinging light

bulb. It clearly had been cut with a sharp knife in three strokes.

"Sabotage," I said.

Cowboy pushed his glasses up. They needed a cleaning.

"They's more'n that, too. I got somethin' at the house to show you. Be right back." And he left us to our investigation.

Edwina traced the break with a wrapped nail-polished orchid pink. "This is outrageous. I didn't think there were vandals this far out in the country."

"We're not looking at the random work of vandals, dear. Someone wanted to put me away. Personally."

"You're just being paranoiac, Matty. Everyone likes you. They must have been aiming for someone else. Maybe me. It was my saddle."

"Cowboy doesn't think so." I picked up the strap again and then felt a chill so icy that I shook. And it wasn't the night wind blowing off the swamp. "Hold on, Edwina. I just remembered something Roy Robicheaux said: A man who knows animals would never turn his back on one he isn't acquainted with."

She was examining her saddle for further damage. ."I guess he wouldn't."

"Especially if the animal was wild and dangerous."

"I should say not."

I grabbed her arm. "We've got to get out of here!"

She dropped the saddle panel. "But why?"

"Because I am one stupid queer, that's why." I made for the door, pulling her along with me. "Do you know who can tie knots as well as riggers and Navy men?"

Edwina shook her head, but then the answer came from somewhere near a cigarette glow out in the dark.

"Rodeo riders."

Charles Eisenhardt stepped through the doorway, nearly filling it and blocking our way. His thick lenses glinted under the single bulb.

"That's what you were thinkin', wasn't it? A man who ropes calves can tie a pretty good knot."

"More than that, Cowboy. A savvy handler of animals would never turn his back on a grizzly."

He grinned widely. "No. I wouldn't."

"So how did you get those bruises on the backs of your legs?"

"You tell me."

"When you hanged poor Brad, you just slung him over your back while he kicked his life away, didn't you?"

"Wasn't nothin' else to hang him on."

"And he kicked hard."

"He did that. He sure did. Though it was his own dern fault. If he'd given up that paper, I wouldna had to be so harsh with him."

"But it wasn't an option on your land, was it? You never gave him one."

" 'Course not. I made up that story as my excuse to stay in touch with you. Just in case your head cleared up an' you started rememberin'."

"What Brad had was a signed forfeiture of title to our riverfront property. I'd guess you did all this for the heir of Henry Vigé."

"Smart boy. You got it figured, yup."

"It must be Jessica."

"My wife was such an easy mark, too. So trusting she signed that paper without tellin' me 'cause she wanted it for a surprise. You know what that sidewinder gave her for her signature? A paltry five hundred dollars. Five hundred for a title that could be worth millions."

"So you met him to retrieve the title. Naturally, he wouldn't turn it over to you."

"Thought the law was stronger than Cowboy. Awful stupid for an educated man. I saw this here rope laying right there on his coffee table like a gift from the Lord, so I jes' lassoed the hombre like a calf and hanged him up. Then I put the stool in the closet and pulled his britches down so he'd look like he was just jackin' off like those fellas on Channel Six."

"Then you took the title away with you."

"Burned it. And now I'll have to deal with you, Matty. I'm real sorry about that, cuz you never done me any harm. But you know my ladies got to come first." Cowboy spit the cigarette out of his mouth and stomped on it. "I knew Brad was double crossin' his partner on the deal, so I thought only him and me knew about the title. When I figured out that he told you too, I saw a problem. You might shake out of your fit and remember that I had the best reason to kill him."

"You also had the best opportunity to cut through Cricket's girth."

"Thought I might could get lucky. If she throwed you and cracked your head the rest of the way, you wouldn't be much of a botheration."

"But the mare didn't cooperate. She refused to jump where you heaped all that gravel."

"When I saw you walkin' back, I knew I'd have to try again, and tonight was my chance. I jes' had to pick up this here." He reached into his coat pocket and pulled out a pearl-handled revolver in case I decided to fight him, which would have been unthinkable in any case. "At least you won't have to die in that sissy flowered shirt you was wearin' first time I saw you."

So he had remembered that incident after all these years.

I was mortified.

"See, Matt, tonight I planned a simple little accident for you. You was goin' to get stomped to death by Cricket whilst she was in one of her moods." He swung the gun around his finger by the trigger guard. "But now who's gonna believe she stomped the both o' y'all. That's a complication."

Edwina put her hands on her hips. "Well, now I'm sorry I came!"

"Me too, gal. Cause I didn't want to get you involved. I sure never killed a woman before."

"You're going to shoot us?"

"No, that'd be kinda hard to explain. Shot people get to look shot, see. Just you take that path there and move your butts."

As we walked ahead of him, Edwina clung to me, shivering and tripping over the sticks and shells on the path. "For heaven's sake, if I'd known we were going for a hike, I wouldn't have worn heels."

"Don't worry about it now," I said.

"But these are my best Roger Vivier pumps!"

"I'll buy you a new pair."

"You *are* going to get us out of this, aren't you?"

It was a command.

"Yes, dear." I turned without slowing my pace. "Listen, Cowboy. This was all for nothing. Jessica's title is no good."

He didn't slow down either, or lower his revolver.

"Brad tol' me y'all ancestor's first wife was a colored woman. Their kids were bastards."

"But that man, Francis Vigé, was one-sixteenth Negro. He was colored, too."

"What's that mean?"

"His marriage to my great-great-great grandmother was legal. The marriage to Jessica's white ancestor was miscegenation. She has no claim to any Vigé property and never did."

"You musta done some powerful digging in history."

"I did."

"But . . ." He grinned. "Maybe whoever we fight in court won't be so goldern smart as you. Anyhow, I got nothin' to lose tonight."

I spent several more minutes in serious cogitation until Cowboy halted the procession. At the grizzly's den.

He pulled open the door to the absent female's half of the bear cage. "Git in."

Edwina held back. "Matty, aren't you going to fight him?"

"That would be a brief and bloody spectacle. No, I'm not."

I might have outrun the big man and upset his alibi by forcing him to stop me with a bullet. And he knew it. But he also knew that I wouldn't take off and leave a woman to die here alone. I took Edwina's chilly hand and led her into the cage.

Cowboy slammed the door after us and secured it with a padlock. "What happened here is that y'all was feelin' romantic. So you jes' decided to come out here and make love."

"Us?"

"You was feelin' close to nature and all that, and y'all thought, Wouldn't it be fun to do it in a bear cage."

Edwina stamped her dainty foot. "That's the silliest thing I ever heard. I never did it in a cage in my life! . . . Well, not a *bear* cage."

"Figger you thought the connectin' gate was locked and the ol' boy couldn't get at you. But those kind of smells get a bear real excited, so this one woke up and came to see what it was about." He shrugged. "When you knew somethin', it was too late to get out, and there was a real bad accident. I'll jes' take this padlock off when it's over, and we'll all have a good cry."

Edwina trembled. "He's going to bring that bear in here to eat us?"

" 'Fraid so."

Cowboy armed himself with a broomstick and unlocked the door to the adjoining cage. "Y'all won't be bored too long. Yer gettin' company."

He knocked loudly on the wall of the concrete den until the huge, half-ton grizzly lumbered out, a hulking shadow in the moonlight, angry and puzzled at having his rest disturbed.

"Take my advice. It'll be easier if you don't fight him. Jes' go limp and he'll do it quick for you."

He used his stick to poke the grizzly and guided him toward the door connecting the cages.

"Come on, ol' boy. Yer fixin' to git a late supper tonight."

I'm a fairly good climber, so I had a chance of getting up the side of the cage. But not Edwina. The eternal optimist.

"Maybe it won't be hungry."

"It doesn't have to be hungry. Just—" Then I shook her arm and whispered. "Quick! Your Tampax!"

"Wha?" But there was only that second's hesitation. Then, to her infinite credit, my blushing lady just squatted and had it out in the next, and the wad of cotton was warm and wet in my hand.

Edwina ducked away from my throwing arm as I weighed the sanguine missile, calculated trajectory, aimed, and pitched. I have a good eye and put the thing right where I wanted it. Smack into the grizzly's nose. The bear flinched at first, then sniffed at the potent combination of blood and hormones in disbelief. The man realized what had happened before the animal did, but there was no time to escape. The grizzly roared his fury then directed it at the only living creature within reach.

I clambered up the side of the cage, hoisted Edwina over the top and down to safety, then dropped to the ground to hold her tight against me while the battle raged.

Cowboy was right. It would have gone easier if he hadn't fought—and if he hadn't been so strong. I prayed the bear would tear his head off first so the suffering would be over. And I wouldn't have to look at his face. But there was no such mercy. It took the big man a long time to die as the grizzly gave him a grotesque hug that slowly broke his back. He was too proud to cry out until the last second, and then there was breath only for a low, sad sigh as he died on the ground.

Edwina was shaking hard in my arms.

"What happened? Is he dead?"

"He didn't have a chance. Cowboy just met the only critter in town badder than he was."

We hiked back to the house, where I phoned the St. Tammany Parish sheriff, who was on the scene within ten minutes. There was no ambiguity about the case. The bear and the bloody pieces of his handler were still locked in the cage together when the men from the Audubon Zoo came with their tranquilizer darts.

Someone wondered what Edwina and I were doing there, and we said we'd stopped by to discuss Cricket's estrus cycle.

The worst part was the widows who came later, all three of them bent and sobbing with grief. I held Jessica a long time for the little good it did her.

What I didn't tell them was that Cowboy had murdered Brad Rutledge. My knowledge would only be seen as surmise anyhow, and there's no point in trying a dead man.

Death by mishap. If they had any better idea, let them prove it.

The sheriff might have figured that I knew more than I was telling, but they let us go after an hour of debriefing at the scene and signing a statement.

Chapter 21
Monday Night, March 13th

Robin was waiting in the vestibule when I got home. He handed me my nightcap without a word, then let me finish it before speaking.

"You're awfully late. I was worried sick."

"With good reason. Tonight I realized much too late that it was Cowboy who killed Brad Rutledge."

"He hung him up in the closet?"

"Right. And if I didn't have rags for brains, I would have figured it out much sooner," I said on my way to the bedroom. Robin had turned my gas heater on and it was invitingly warm. "There aren't many men strong enough to hang some poor soul in midair. And the bruise he showed me on his leg was already green, so I should have known it wasn't fresh from that morning."

I shucked my clothes and Robin came behind me, picking them up and folding them as I fell into bed without benefit of pajamas.

"By the way, Edwina is inviting you to her wedding."

He froze, with my trousers in his hand. "Her wedding? Me? What about you?"

"Well, I'll be center stage. I'm giving the bride away."

He laughed then, too loudly. Incredulously. "Giving her away?"

"Who else should have the honor? Her father is gone, and I'm the closest she has to a brother. Besides, I have the clothes for it."

"You'll look wonderful walking her down the aisle,

215

Matty. Perfect. I was afraid you were planning to be the groom."

"That arrangement wouldn't have worked. Edwina thought she wanted a Sinclair who would scintillate at parties." I flipped off the reading lamp. "But what she really wants is a good man who will throw healthy children and love her without reservation. She'll have that with Bill Oakes." I patted the pillow next to me. "If she ever gets a yen for skilled lovemaking, she may call on me. So may he, for that matter."

Robin sighed as though he'd just been relieved of a gut pain. Then he hung up my pants and slipped under the covers beside me. "So you're not taking Ondine's advice."

"No, I'm taking Polonius's advice."

"Who?"

"As stated in *Hamlet*. It goes, 'And this above all: To thine own self be true. For thence it must follow as the night the day, thou canst be false to no man.'"

Robin lay against me and his soft curls warmed my cheek.

"Oy luff yoo, Spotakiss."